Summertim

It's amazing how much I can glean from listening to one half of a telephone conversation. I hear whisper, whisper, and then, slowly, half sentences . . . Then the penny drops. The realization that my parents are fighting over me, and that neither of them wants me, hits me like a blow in the belly.

This is the start of a long, painful summer for Alex. He has no choice but to go to Yorkshire with his mother and her new partner, away from his friends, his home, and his A level studies. He just knows he is going to hate it all, the isolation and quiet of the countryside, the cold, primitive cottage, and most of all, Seth. His one thought is to get away, back to civilization in London. But then he meets Louie, who looks after abandoned and ill-treated animals, and Faye, Seth's daughter, and suddenly the summer is full of new experiences and challenges which will change Alex's life for ever.

Julia Clarke was born in Surrey, England, but spent most of her childhood in Germany and Canada. After leaving school at 16, her love of books led to work in a library. After A levels, she gained a Certificate of Education at Goldsmiths College, University of London. A postgraduate course in drama at the Guildford School of Acting was followed by work in all branches of the theatre including writing and performing educational shows in schools. In between acting jobs she travelled to Afghanistan and India, worked for an astrologer and as a cook on a Scottish island. While appearing at Harrogate Theatre, North Yorkshire, she met her husband, Michael, a journalist. They have two teenage children. Julia started writing while living on an isolated farm when her children were small. In 1999 she gained a Distinction in an MA in Creative Writing from University of Leeds. She enjoys keeping animals, walking and going to the theatre. *Summertime Blues*, which is set near her home, is her first novel for Oxford University Press.

Summertime Blues

Julia Clarke

OXFORD
UNIVERSITY PRESS

To my daughter, Bethany, whose help and enthusiasm
kept me writing, with much love.

OXFORD
UNIVERSITY PRESS

Great Clarendon Street, Oxford OX2 6DP

Oxford University Press is a department of the University of Oxford.
It furthers the University's objective of excellence in research, scholarship,
and education by publishing worldwide in

Oxford New York

Athens Auckland Bangkok Bogotá Buenos Aires Calcutta
Cape Town Chennai Dar es Salaam Delhi Florence Hong Kong Istanbul
Karachi Kuala Lumpur Madrid Melbourne Mexico City Mumbai
Nairobi Paris São Paulo Shanghai Singapore Taipei Tokyo Toronto Warsaw

and associated companies in Berlin Ibadan

Oxford is a registered trade mark of Oxford University Press
in the UK and in certain other countries

Copyright © Julia Clarke 2001

The moral rights of the author have been asserted

Database right Oxford University Press (maker)

First published 2001

British Library Cataloguing in Publication Data available

ISBN 0 19 271871 1

1 3 5 7 9 10 8 6 4 2

Typeset by AFS Image Setters Ltd, Glasgow

Printed in Great Britain by Biddles Ltd
Guildford and King's Lynn

Prelude

My mother always waits until she's in the middle of a domestic task before she talks to me about anything important. I swear that if my father ever drops down dead at work she'll wait until she's wrestling with a duvet cover before she tells me.

Our one and only talk about sex (which she called the facts of life) was when I was about nine years old. We still lived out at Watford then; I remember it was a warm summer day and I wanted to go out and play cricket in the park with my mates, but she called me into the kitchen.

'I really wanted your father to have a little talk with you, man-to-man,' she said, really snappily, and I immediately sensed a row between my parents in the making. 'But as he can't do it. I will.'

As she said this she squirted a great whoosh of washing-up liquid into the sink and ran some scalding water. Then she pulled on her rubber gloves, as if she was some kind of mad doctor, and launched into a tirade of biological facts about babies and wombs. As she talked

1

she agitated the detergent in the sink into a great mass of bubbles and began dunking glasses as if her life depended on it. By the time she got on to the interesting bits she was using a scouring pad on the roasting tin, her face red and hot as she rubbed and scrubbed. And I was watching the bubbles in the sink, they were as high as the taps and still growing.

'There!' she said, inspecting the gleaming tin. 'I hope you found that informative. Any questions?'

'Yes, can I go and play now?' I asked. She gave me a look of exasperation and disbelief and I knew I'd said the wrong thing, but I scooted out before she could tell me anything else. Her clinical descriptions weren't anywhere near as exciting as the stuff we talked about in the playground: she'd made sex sound about as interesting as gardening.

Later, she waited until she was cooking before telling me that she and Dad were getting divorced. Once again she called me into the kitchen, where she was beating steak and chopping onions, and I remember her short sharp sentences running in rhythm with the clatter of the knife.

'Your father and I have decided to call it a day. It must be obvious. Even to you. How bad things are between us. We've only stayed together for your sake.'

It's amazing how your parents can make you feel guilty about something which has nothing to do with you. I didn't ask them to get married, or to have me, or to live together in misery for seventeen years. I'm just an innocent bystander.

My parents' divorce didn't make much difference to my life at first. Dad moved out immediately so I didn't see him leave. I just came home to find the dining-room clear of his Apple Mac and fax machine: it was only then I realized how little time he had been spending with us, because I hardly missed him.

Little things got on my nerves though—like when he

asked me to call him Steve instead of Dad: I ended up not calling him anything at all. And it was the same with my mother; I really didn't mind her being wild and weepy, or spending hours on the phone, what did upset me was when she 'changed her image'.

Before the divorce she'd worked part-time for a solicitor and worn long navy skirts and blouses with ruffled necklines. But she jacked that job in, got another with a television company, and began to dress like a tart. I was gobsmacked. Then I got angry. It was awful seeing her in a mini-skirt and black tights . . . worse still in a tight jumper with an uplift bra underneath.

Eventually I stopped inviting anyone to our house because it was too incredibly embarrassing. As well as dressing as if she were sweet sixteen she got all giggly and girlish too—and started staying out late.

At that time I thought having an adolescent-retard mother was about as bad as things could get, but I didn't know the half of it! Parents keep all kinds of little surprises up their sleeves. After a while she started not coming home at all. It was weird. There I was, coming up seventeen, the right age for teenage rebellion and wild living. Stuff that! I was spending long evenings in my room studying hard for A levels, living a life which would have made a monastery look exciting, while my mother was out on the town.

At first I told myself it was cool having the house to myself. But soon I began to hate the echoing emptiness when I came home; the sour unlived-in smell of the sitting-room, which we didn't use any more, and eating stuff straight from the microwave. The whole house seemed to groan with neglect. It was making me feel really fed up—and I was getting ready to tell my mother so—when the telephone conversations started.

1

It's amazing how much I can glean from listening to one half of a telephone conversation. Not that I deliberately eavesdrop on her. It's just she does shout when she gets upset. So I hear whisper, whisper and then, slowly, half sentences: 'I do more than my fair share. I have a life to lead. You are his father. Doesn't need a lot of room. Don't tell me what I can and can't do.'

Then the penny drops. The realization that my parents are fighting over me, and that neither of them wants me, hits me like a blow in the belly. A hot pain starts somewhere below my ribs and I begin to feel a bit sick. It's no good trying to kid myself the pizza I heated for supper might have been off, because there is a tell-tale heat suffusing my face, my hands are shaky and I want to smash something. I've got a bad dose of parent-rage—not food poisoning.

Lots of crazy thoughts race through my mind; but I realize that most of them, including death or desertion, would be playing right into my parents' hands. And at that moment I feel like making life hard for them, not easy.

With an attempt at careless nonchalance I wander into the kitchen and take a can of Coke from the fridge. My mother finishes the phone conversation abruptly and starts flapping around, getting the ironing board from the under-stairs cupboard.

'Have you anything which needs ironing, Alex?' she asks, filling the iron at the tap. I shake my head. 'I am going up to Yorkshire for a while,' she says, in a really huffy tone, as if expecting me to argue with her.

'Cool,' I say, sitting down at the table and watching her shake out a skimpy white T-shirt and start ironing.

'You can't miss school so you can stay with your father until the holidays start and then, if you wanted to, you can come up to Yorkshire and stay with me. But it *is* out in the country.' This is said as if being out in the country is the ultimate deterrent, like bubonic plague or chemical warfare.

'Cool,' I say again, and she darts this beady look at me, as if not sure whether I am serious or not.

'Who are you going with?'

'Someone I've been seeing for a while.' She is thumping and sizzling that T-shirt like it's trying to get away from her. It's funny—her clothes are so skimpy yet they take so much ironing. Holding the shirt up she looks at it critically, then attacks it again, pressing her thumb down, spraying water and thudding the iron on some tiny little crease. No one else in the world would see that microscopic wrinkle—but my mother has.

'Yeah,' I say encouragingly, because I have to admit I'm curious.

'He's an actor. His name's Seth McElroy.' And she shoots this little look at me, as if expecting me to know the name.

That's when I do this big act of being really knocked out and surprised: 'Jeez . . . No! You don't mean to tell me . . . It can't be true! You're not dating *the* Seth McElroy? Wow!'

It's pathetic! She gives me this coy little look and smiles with pleasure. And if I wasn't so angry with her I could almost feel sorry for kidding her about something which is obviously important.

'You know him?' she says tentatively. 'What have you seen him in?'

'Seen him? Have I? What does he do? Toothpaste

commercials?' Finishing the Coke I crunch the can with one hand, because I know this annoys her.

When I glance up she is giving me this really hard look. 'You can go over to your father's this evening and sort everything out.'

'What's happening about your job?' I ask, in a more conciliatory tone.

'I've got a six month transfer to Yorkshire Television as a production assistant. But, if things go well, I may stay up there.' Not even her ill-temper with me can hide the gleeful expression in her eyes as she says this.

'Why do you want to go and live in Yorkshire?' I ask, but she has started ironing some trousers and completely ignores me. Even when I go up to my room and play my music at top volume she still ignores me. I haven't seen my father in months but curiosity gets the better of me. Pulling on my jacket I leave the house without speaking to her, making sure I slam the front door so she knows I've left: but there is just silence from the kitchen.

My father lives in a really grotty flat in north London. When he left us he lived on his own for about two weeks. Then his secretary, Mandy, moved in with him. I think it was all planned and the two weeks was an attempt to throw us off the scent. I used to like his secretary before she moved in with Dad. She's only in her twenties and she's really gorgeous looking, a Marilyn Monroe look-alike. Mum says she's a brainless bimbo. So I just keep quiet about her now. When she was just Dad's secretary my friend Danny and I used to have quite a crush on her and say things like: 'Wouldn't throw her out of bed for eating monkey nuts,' but I can't do that now. If I'm really honest the idea of Mandy and Dad getting it together makes me feel a bit sick.

Dad and Mandy took me out a few times to begin with. It was really weird. I mean Dad and I had never spent much time together and then, suddenly, we were expected to spend the whole of Saturday being chummy. We went to the cinema and to McDonald's a couple of times but it got me really depressed. Mandy and Dad hold hands all the time and talk to each other in a kind of code. 'All right, sweetie?' he'd say to her. 'Fine and dandy,' she would reply.

Then I suppose they got a bit more relaxed with me, because Dad started coming out with some really soppy stuff: 'Is my baby cold?' he asked her once when we were walking on Hampstead Heath. It was after that I put a stop to the weekend visits. We were running out of places to go, anyway. As I said to Danny, if I wasn't careful I'd end up at the zoo, trailing around with all the other part-time fathers and access kids. The animals must look at us all and think the human race has gone mad.

Mandy opens the door and seems surprised to see me. 'Alex! How lovely to see you. You're quite a stranger.'

I stand on the doorstep for a moment feeling a real fool. Mandy's only about five feet tall and she always makes me feel awkward: as if my arms and legs are too long and my feet too big. I suddenly know that whatever my parents are planning Mandy knows nothing about it. And I also realize, with a hot flush of embarrassment, that Mandy is pregnant. She has kind of ballooned and everything about her is rounded and sticking out: she has fat little cheeks now, a dimple in her chin and huge water-melon breasts with a big lump jutting out underneath. Also she's wearing dungaree things which show the bump off, like she's really proud of it.

'I've been meaning to ring you and ask you over for a meal,' she says, ushering me into the front room of the flat. Her face has flushed to a blotchy pink and she is nibbling at her lower lip uneasily. 'I'm glad you've dropped by. Will you stop and have something to eat with us? Steve will be home soon, he's working late.'

'Slaving over a hot secretary?' I quip. Mandy laughs, but her baby-blue eyes are filled with sudden hurt and I say quickly, 'Look, I won't wait. I'll come around another time to see him.' I make for the door. But to my horror, Mandy gets hold of my hands and pulls me to a halt.

'We both wanted to see you, Alex. We've got some news. I mean I really wanted Steve to be the one to tell you. But as he's not here . . . ' She takes a deep breath, like a kid who is going to tell you an important secret. 'Well . . . You see. We're very happy because we're going to have a baby.' As she says this she flashes me this brilliant smile that almost splits her chubby face in two.

'Yeah, well, I did kind of notice. Congratulations,' I say feebly, pulling away from her.

'Oh,' she says delightedly, running her hands over the sides of the bump and beaming. 'Did you guess? Is it starting to show at last?'

'Just a bit . . . ' I mumble. Jeez! Does it show? She's the size of a barrage balloon. I worry she might give birth at any moment.

'There was nothing to see for ages! I got quite worried. I kept on saying to Steve—where's this baby hiding?' She laughs, and it makes her little double chin wobble. 'He'll make a super dad, won't he, Alex?' she laughs again. I get the feeling that this is a line she has said so often it is like a motto, or maybe brain-washing. And that if she says it often enough she and my father might start to believe it.

The laughter stops abruptly and she is chewing her lip again. Her eyes are suddenly anxious. I don't remind her that he already is a father—and one with a lousy track record at that. Instead I shift uneasily from foot to foot.

'Look, I've got to go,' I say. 'Congratulations on the baby. Let me know when it arrives. I'll go and get something in Mothercare. Do you have a list—like for weddings?'

'Oh, Alex!' she squeals, and bursts into a peal of laughter. 'You are such a sweetheart. Thank you for being pleased!' She throws her arms up around my neck and gives me a hug. It is a totally gross experience. And the worst thing is that it makes me think back to the times before Dad got together with her, when I would have walked a hundred miles for a hug like this. But now I can feel her bump pressing into me and her hair tickling my chin.

Having her so close to me makes me stagger with embarrassment: 'Yeah well, I'll keep in touch. Got to go . . .'

'No you don't!' She is moving me into a chair. 'You must stay and eat with us. I've made a casserole and jacket potatoes. There's masses. Take your jacket off and I'll get you a beer.' Then she starts to tug at my jacket sleeve. 'I'm allowed to bully you now I'm going to be a mother,' she jokes. 'Getting into practice for your little brother or sister.'

To stop her hanging on my arm I give in and take off my jacket. I can hear her banging around in the kitchen, singing to herself. Suddenly I realize I have managed to make her happy. Goodness knows how.

When my father arrives I can see he is in a bad mood, although he tries to hide it by slapping my shoulder and asking me about school. Then he leaves me nursing my warm beer and follows Mandy into the kitchen. When they call me in to eat I guess by her face that he has told her unwelcome news: she looks like a kid whose dog has died.

'I hear your mother is going up to Yorkshire. That will be nice,' Mandy says carefully, as she dishes up the food. Everything in the flat is geared for a couple and they have only a tiny table and two chairs in the kitchen. My father is perched uncomfortably on a bar stool.

'I have to apologize to you, Alex,' she says bravely. 'Because I know when we moved in here we showed you the back bedroom and told you it was your room. But . . . as you never came to stay I've got it ready for the baby.'

'It doesn't matter . . . ' my father says irritably, spearing a chunk of meat and frowning at it.

'It does matter, Stephen,' Mandy says pertly. 'We told Alex he had a home and a bedroom here. And it was true, is true. Only I've painted the room, Alex . . . So, I'm sorry, you'll have to live with Jemima Puddleduck and friends for a few weeks.' And she gives me this really lovely smile. I find myself smiling back: because even though she is so fat she's still very pretty.

'Look, it's very kind of you, Mand,' I say, deliberately using a nickname I know my father doesn't like. 'But I don't need to come and stay with you just because Mum is away. I'll be fine on my own.'

For the first time since he arrived back from his office my father looks into my eyes. 'Hasn't she told you?' he asks quietly.

'Told me?' I parrot back to him. The casserole, which minutes ago had been so delicious, suddenly is like gravel in my mouth. When I swallow my mouthful it seems to get stuck somewhere in my chest.

'Your mother is renting out the house to some Americans. You can't stay there . . . ' he says flatly.

Before I can stop myself I glance at Mandy and see pity in her eyes. 'But you are more than welcome to come here to us,' she says quickly. 'The spare room is lovely now. There's a new wardrobe and chest-of-drawers. And there's room for a desk . . . ' She is rattling on like an express train.

Looking down at the plate of meat and vegetables before me on the table I notice that the butter has melted into a glistening, golden puddle. It is the first decent bit of home-cooked grub I've had in weeks. In a moment of savage anger I wish my bloody father had waited until I'd finished eating before telling me about my mother's plans. I'm still hungry but I know even a forkful of spud would choke me now. As I push the plate away I see that Mandy is looking stricken, as if she might cry. If my father wasn't here then we might have cried together.

2

My mother leaves me a note in the kitchen telling me she is coming to the school concert. Then my father phones and says he and Mandy are also coming along. This is seriously weird because normally they take turns to attend events like parents' evening. I can't help worrying there will be a scene, because my mother has not come face to face with Mandy since she moved in with Dad. Really I am too fed up to care very much, I just don't want to be embarrassed in front of my friends.

When I try to talk to my mother about me staying in the house she starts crying and says things like: 'I have to have my chance of happiness too, you know.' As if I am trying to spoil her life or something.

The thought of being stuck in a tiny flat with my father and Mandy makes my hands sweat with nerves. I can't imagine getting up in the morning and having breakfast with them: Mandy in a pink dressing-gown and fluffy slippers, pouring coffee for my father and kissing him goodbye. I will go crazy.

Eventually I tell Danny about it. He is my best mate and he offers to ask his mum if I can kip in their spare room. I know Danny's parents aren't well off so I offer to pay for my board and lodging. If my mother won't cough up I can take it out of my bank account.

Because I have to stay at school and rehearse I don't see my mother before the concert, but I know when she comes into the hall because Danny's face changes. At first, when I look up, I can only see his parents. Danny's parents are real old hippies and I used to feel sorry for him. But not any more. His mum is wearing some droopy 1960's dress, which is covered with flowers and comes down to her ankles, and her hair flows down her back like a browny-grey river. His dad is wearing faded denims that are so grubby and wrinkled they look like elephant skin, and his hair is tied back in a ponytail. But they look really ordinary and comforting next to my mother and her partner.

Shrinking my head down between my shoulders, like a tortoise being troubled by a dog, I suddenly find that all those corny old phrases like—'I wanted the ground to open and swallow me up'—are horribly accurate. If wishes could come true I would wish to be anywhere in the world rather than here.

Inside my brain I can hear my mother's voice saying that she has made a real effort this evening. Whether it's for this new fella or to impress Mandy I don't know or care. All I know is that she's done up like a dog's dinner.

'Cor, who's that? Right bit of crumpet . . . ' the saxophonist next to me says.

'Shut it, pillock brain,' Danny hisses.

'Leave it out, that's my mother,' I mumble, and the boy stifles a giggle.

'Is that your dad?' he asks.

'No . . . ' I say bleakly. What a stupid question. Would my mother be done up like a sailor's comfort if she was out with my father?

My mother minces down the hall, she is wearing outrageously high heels and stockings with seams. A ridiculous little hat is perched on her blonde hair. She looks like an extra from *Bugsy Malone*. This is what you get from mixing with actors.

Mandy and Dad arrive at about the same time, they sit at the opposite side of the hall and I can see Mandy craning her neck to get a look at my mother. I feel as if everyone in the hall is looking at her. Half of them probably don't recognize her because she doesn't look anything like she used to. When she takes off her jacket I close my eyes to block out the sight of her skimpy lacy blouse and stomach-turning cleavage.

'Hey! I know the guy your mother is with,' the kid next to me says. 'He plays a cop in *Killers*. He's really good.'

Danny and I exchange glances. All I can think is that the people who aren't staring at my mother are staring at Seth McElroy wondering where they've seen him before.

What with one thing and another, I play really badly during the concert, even though normally I'm quite good on the old sax. At one point I lose it completely and feel the conductor's beady eye on me as I fumble and drone. This could be my last performance with the orchestra, which, if my mother is planning to come to any more concerts with lover boy, is just as well.

After the concert the parents of people in the orchestra hang around at the back of the hall while we put away our instruments. I spend ages cleaning the spit out of my sax and try to avoid looking at my mother. A group of first-year girls—the knock-kneed nerdy types with specs—are hanging around Seth McElroy, flapping bits of paper ripped from their homework diaries and asking for his autograph.

Danny and I exchange looks again. The good thing about having a best mate is that sometimes you don't need to say anything. Our glances say all too clearly: pass the sick bag. These kids are obviously the type who watch every drop of trash that is spewed out of the TV. Seth McElroy doesn't look like anything special to me and I certainly don't recognize his face. He is quite short and dark with slicked-back hair and a four-o'clock shadow on his jaw. He is dressed in a severe double-breasted pin-striped suit with a gangster hat and he and my mother obviously think they look like Bonnie and Clyde.

Why they couldn't have come along in jeans and anoraks and blended in with the rest of the parents beats me. I am absolutely furious with my mother; when she teeters across to me making a kissing face, I pull away from her hand like a badly trained dog. Seth McElroy pumps my arm and tells me what a fine sax player I am. As this is so obviously untrue I mutter something about having a bad evening and hunch my shoulders. My mother is talking about going out for a pizza.

For the first time in my life I wish that I was a girl. Because I can't think of an excuse for not going with them and girls can always get away with a headache or period pains. I try saying I've got a lot of work to do, but Seth McElroy slaps my shoulder and tells me I need a beer and to unwind.

Dad and Mandy come over and I turn away so I don't have to watch my mother hanging on to Seth McElroy's arm and giving Mandy a cheesy smile. I hate them all at that moment. Then, through the throng of people, I see Danny's dad making a beeline for us. With a surge of panic I realize he is coming over to talk to my mother about me staying in their spare room and I feel my face growing red and sweaty.

Danny's dad is all right, but weird. He has this great big moustache which flops down over his mouth. It looks as if he uses it to filter his food and quite often has things stuck in it. And it doesn't do to speculate what they are, or how long they've been there, especially at meal times. He also has two very chipped grey teeth in the front of his mouth, which Danny says he got from falling off a motorbike. These are things I know my mother will notice immediately. She's always going on about teeth and getting rid of spots and 'presenting a nice face to the world'. The moustache is the kind of thing which really turns her stomach. She will take one look and make all kinds of assumptions about Danny's folks.

Backing away from the group I intercept him before he

reaches them. I can hear Mandy laughing, she does it a lot when she is nervous. 'Hi, Mr Smith,' I say to Danny's dad. 'What did you think of the concert?'

He gives me this really sad look, like a poor old walrus that hasn't caught a fish in months. 'It was great, really great,' he says. 'You want to practise that sax, you'll be good on it one day. I was going to talk to your ma about you staying with us.' He goes to move around me, but I sidestep and block his path.

'She's a bit busy right now,' I say desperately. He is chewing at his moustache, the middle of it is quite wet and I watch enthralled as he sucks it in and then releases it.

'OK. I'll talk to her some other time. When you've had a chance to tell her what you've got planned.' The fact that he has seen so clearly what the score is, makes me suddenly feel humble. He may look like some hopeless old dead-beat but he knows what is happening in people's hearts.

'Thanks, Mr Smith,' I say gratefully.

'Who was that?' asks my mother, as Danny's dad slopes back across the hall, his Indian sandals flapping on the hardwood floor.

'He's the peripatetic music tutor. He was talking to me about an extra rehearsal,' I lie glibly.

'Really?' she says, watching Mr Smith's retreating back. I know she is noticing that the seat of his jeans are baggy and none too clean.

'Yeah, well, don't judge a book by its cover. He used to play with Ronnie Scott.' The words are out before I can stop them. Jeez! I don't know why I have told such a big useless lie, because I used to be a very truthful person and pride myself on not needing to make up stupid stories like some of the kids at school. But being angry with my mother seems to have started some kind of rot inside me and I can't control it.

'You should have introduced him to Seth then,' she says with a smile.

Muttering an excuse I go off to the bog with my saxophone. I have this insane thought that I might climb out of the window and get away from my mother. It's an incredibly stupid idea because the windows open only a fraction.

When I come out I see Seth McElroy talking to Mandy and I hear her laugh rising shrilly. My parents are deep in discussion. And the idea comes to me in a flash that I can turn my back on them and go.

It's like a statement I want to make to the world. That I don't care about either of them and I don't want to hang around with them. But, to tell the truth, I'm shaking like a junkie as I do it. It's the fear of being caught that gives me the shivers. It would just be so embarrassing trying to explain why I am sneaking away. As I slip out through the double glass doors I keep thinking I hear my mother's voice calling out my name.

When I get outside the school there is this kid standing on the kerb crying. I stop and stare for a moment at her long plaits tied up with ribbons and her pale little face. I know it's utter madness to stop and speak to her, but I put my saxophone down and crouch so I can peer at her. She doesn't look anywhere near old enough to be at secondary school.

'What's the problem?' I ask, in what I hope is a suitably sympathetic voice. She turns her head away and doesn't answer. 'Haven't your parents come for you?' I enquire.

'I thought my daddy was going to come to the concert. But I didn't see him. Maybe he thought Mummy was coming . . .'

Another happy family, I think to myself, as I reach for her flute case. 'Let's go along to the office and ring your mum,' I suggest.

Sniffing, she hands me the case and follows me back into the school. Through the open door I can see my parents, still talking.

The office is closed but I take the kid up to the sixth form common room and use the pay phone. I promise her mother I will stay with the kid, who is called Nina, until she arrives. I get us both a hot chocolate and a Twix from the self-service machine and she sits on one of the crummy chairs we have in the common room and swings her legs. Now she's got to know me she doesn't stop talking . . . I find it relaxing listening to her. All I have to do is nod or say 'yes' or 'wow' at intervals. It takes her ages to finish the hot chocolate and when we get downstairs everyone has gone and the caretaker is putting away the chairs.

The mother offers me a lift, but I would rather walk. As they drive away Nina turns around and waves at me, beaming a toothy radiant smile, like I'm a hero or something. And for the first time since finding out that Mandy is pregnant I am a little bit pleased about it.

There is no one at home but there is an angry message on the answerphone for me from my mother. She sounds as if she has drunk a couple of glasses of wine too quickly before phoning me. Wiping the message off the tape, I unplug the phone and go to bed. I hear my mother come in at around two o'clock. She tries the handle of my bedroom door but I've locked it.

Even though my mother cooks a Sunday lunch I spend the weekend locked in my room. I wait until she has gone out and then I get the joint from the fridge. Picking bits of meat and cold potatoes from the dish I eat them standing up in the middle of the kitchen. And all the time I can hear her voice inside my head saying things like: 'Don't eat standing up. We're not having lunch on the hoof. Sit down, you'll ruin your digestion.' And I am pleased I am doing something she wouldn't approve of.

That is my only attempt at rebellion because I have to write an essay on George Eliot for my English tutor and I don't intend to let my work slip. I keep thinking how good it will be to get away to uni and get a flat. The one thing in the world I want is to do really well in my exams.

The essay comes out fantastically well. I'm really pleased with it and confident of at least a B and maybe even an A. The other really brilliant thing is that Danny comes into school with this big grin on his face and says: 'Ma says she'd love to have you staying. And, if you don't want to go up to Yorkshire for the holidays, you can come camping with us. As long as you don't mind sharing a tent with me. We're going to Sark again. It's a great place.'

Relief comes over me like a sense of physical warmth. It's as if the sun has suddenly come out from behind a cloud. I could almost hug Danny. He's really saved me. 'Thanks, mate. I'll think about the tent. How many pairs of socks are you taking?' I say, and we end up pushing each other and laughing.

We go into German together and I'm in a really good mood. I feel almost high with relief that I will not have to stay with Mandy and Dad, or spend the summer with my mother and Seth McElroy. I'm doing sums in my head. I have loads of money in my bank account because both my parents give me an allowance. Which means I could probably afford to buy my own tent, and maybe Danny and I could go over to France on our own for a bit.

We have a new student who has come to help us with conversational German. She's a willowy blonde, with a flawless skin, and all the boys have pushed their way to the front and are sitting staring at her. The girls have mutinously gathered in the back rows. Danny and I sit in the second row. Fräulein Wilhelm is obviously nervous and moves around the class talking to each of us. She asks the same questions over and over again. It's the kind of thing we did in the first year and is really boring.

'Excuse me, Fräulein,' one of the girls says pertly. 'We are an A level group. We normally discuss politics or literature in conversation class.'

'Speak in German, please,' Fräulein says, in English.

The girl titters. It is my turn to speak but I'm not really listening because I know what she will ask. I feel sorry for the Fräulein, her cheeks are rather pink and she's getting flustered.

We go through all the details of who I am and what I am interested in. When it gets to who I live with, the words: 'I live with my mother', somehow stick in my throat. They conjure up the picture of some sad old git of about fifty who never got himself a life and so ends up living with his mother. So instead I say I live with my *Vater*, which considering my father's digestive system is pretty accurate.

Then she asks me if I have any brothers or sisters. For a split second Mandy's bump comes into my mind, but I don't think a foetus which is actually the illegitimate child of your father's secretary counts.

'*Ich bin einzelkind*,' I mutter.

The Fräulein is standing so close to me I can smell the peppery scent of her cologne, and see the rise and fall of her breasts under her white tunic top as she breathes; but she has not heard my words, probably because the girls at the back have started to talk and giggle.

'*Einzelkind?*' she questions.

'*Ja!*' I say, too loudly. '*Ich bin einzelkind.*'

The boy in front of me is called Palmer. He's an OK bloke. Not that I've ever been too friendly with him, but we were in the footie team together and he once invited me to a party at his house. I've never really liked or disliked him.

Now he leans back in his chair and turns to grin at me. 'You may be an only child but you've got a very nice mother,' he says, as if this is a really funny thing to say.

For a second my rational brain tells me that he's just being blokish and I should laugh it off or agree with him. You know: 'Nice mum,' nod, nod, wink, wink. But there is something about his grin and the glint in his eyes that makes me really angry. My eyes lock with his and it's like he is being lost in a red cloud.

The next thing I know I have him off his chair and over my desk and the Fräulein is screaming. From somewhere, beyond the fog which has enveloped my brain, I hear Danny yelling my name. That's the only thing which brings me to my senses.

Looking around, the first thing I notice is that the front of the Fräulein's white top is splattered with thick goblets of scarlet, like poppies. The red is very vivid against the white; for some crazy reason it reminds me of a carol we used to sing called 'The Holly and the Ivy'. When I look down at my hand, which is throbbing, I see that it too has red on it, but watery red, like powder paint mixed too thin.

All around is noise and mayhem. The girls are gathering, Kleenex in their hands, the crowd parts and I see Palmer huddled over his desk. His nose is bleeding like a fountain. Jeez! the guy must be haemophilic or something. I'd hate to be around if he ever cuts himself shaving—he'd need a transfusion.

'You bleed like an effing pig!' I snarl at him, and Danny grabs hold of my arms and marches me out of the room.

'For goodness' sake, Alex!' he yells at me. 'What's the matter with you? A prat like Palmer makes some stupid crack and you go off like Terminator Two. You'll get yourself expelled if you start hitting people for no reason—you effing idiot!'

Danny and I have been best mates for six years and I've never seen him like this—all angry and upset at the same time.

'Did I hit him hard?' I ask lamely.

'Hit him hard?' Danny is marching me along the corridor towards the sixth form common room. 'You flattened his cruddy nose! What on earth were you thinking of? I mean you could have waited and given him a mouthful outside. You didn't have to do it in the classroom. That Fräulein is just about to wet her knickers.'

There is no one else in the sixth form room. Danny puts some cold wet paper towels on my hand and gets me a black coffee from the machine. Firstly I start to shiver, then I begin to feel really ill, as if I'm getting flu. And all the time I am submerged in this weird feeling—as if none of this is actually happening to me. It's like I am watching myself from a distance.

Eventually I have to watch myself in the headmaster's study. There I see a caricature of me: sullen-faced, shoulders slumped, eyes glued to the carpet while I get roasted. The only thing which hurts me is when he says 'the incident' will have to go on my record card and could affect my chances of getting into the university of my choice. When he tells me to go home, I go. There's not much else I can do.

As I am walking away from school I toy with the idea of going to my father's flat and trying to see Mandy. My hand really hurts and I would like someone to fuss over it, maybe bathe it and put ointment on the grazes. This desire turns into a little fantasy about Mandy looking after my hand and then hugging me better. But, even in my shocked state, I can see that it would be a creepy thing to do. And although I crave company I go straight home.

When I get back to the house I open all the windows and put on some loud music. Then I chop onions and start to cook a meal. Spag bol with lots of garlic. I want the house to smell of food and to be like a home again.

3

My father shouts so much he spits. Little specks of froth keep flying out of his mouth. The only way I can handle it is to turn my mind to something else. So I start to think about the language we use to describe temper, and conclude that it is very old-fashioned and to do with weather and stuff like that.

'My father is thundering and roaring, his face is like a black cloud and his words tear into me like shards of rain or hail.' That sounds really naff and I'd never put it in an essay.

Interested in him at last, I watch his mouth working like a trapdoor as I try to think of something more original. 'His words are like a home-made terrorist bomb, nails of rage exploding all around me.' Yes, that's better. It even has a ring of Hemingway about it, I think.

'Are you listening to me?' His face is very close to mine. I smell his breath: cigs and beer and teeth which need cleaning, before I turn my face away. 'Answer me! You stupid little sod!' he spits into my face. I have to stop myself raising my hand and wiping my cheek. For a moment a shiver of fear runs through me.

'Stephen! Please. It won't help!' my mother wails. She's wearing black, as if this is a funeral. This is the first time my father has been back here, to this dusty house which was once our home, and she is decked out in widow's weeds. The effect is rather spoilt by the fact that her long slinky skirt is split to the top of her thighs and her cashmere jumper is a very snug fit. I watch her breasts bouncing as she grabs hold of his arm and pulls him away from me. If only she would buy bigger clothes . . .

'You've had every chance, every advantage . . . ' my father is saying. 'We've done everything we can for you, you ungrateful little sod. You've had music lessons and holidays abroad. I tell you, Sonny Jim, I would have thought I was in effing heaven if I'd had it all when I was your age.'

'Stephen!' my mother wails again. This is what she has got for marrying beneath her. She was not brought up in a household where the F word was ever used. My granny and grandpa probably still don't know what it means. But my father . . . Well, he's rough and ready . . . Black Country poor boy made good.

'You're not even listening to me! Sitting there with that gormless look on your face.' He is struggling in my mother's arms. 'Have you been sniffing something? You stupid little . . . ' The rest of his words are lost as my mother wrestles with him.

Swiftly, sensing real danger, I move to the door: 'I don't know what all the fuss is about. I've only been suspended. I can go back in September. It's not long until the end of term. Loads of people get suspended. There's no need to freak out about it.'

'I suppose you think you're going to sit around the flat and have Mandy waiting on you hand and foot.' He is nearly howling with rage now and he reminds me of some old wolf with his bony face and grizzled blond hair. Since my parents split I'd thought I didn't mind him: you know, take him or leave him, type of thing. Now I know I hate his guts.

'I'm not staying with you and Manders,' I say, opening the door so I can make a quick exit. 'Nothing in the world would induce me to. I've arranged to stay with a friend.'

'No, you're not!' My mother moves quickly and closes the door. 'I've been to see the Smiths and you are definitely not staying with them. Under no circumstances is a son of mine living with that crew!'

If she has been around to see Danny's mum and dad that has really blown it. They live in a council house that is totally scruffy. Danny has two younger sisters and they're really messy. Just for a moment I close my eyes and imagine my mother stepping over all the broken toys and dog's bones which litter the front porch. Did she go into the kitchen? Danny's family have three cats who sit on the work tops and scavenge from the plates waiting to be washed up. My mother hates germs and animals in equal measure. The Smiths' home would be hell on earth to her.

'I think the Smiths' house is fine,' I say mutinously. 'And I don't see that it matters to you—you're not going to be living there. Danny's parents are kind and friendly, the salt of the earth. And Danny's mum is a great cook. She bakes all her own bread. Our house isn't exactly sparkling at the moment, in case you haven't noticed.'

'You haven't eaten around there, have you?' my mother asks, her eyes bulging with disbelief and horror. 'Their kitchen is a health hazard. The dog urinated on the floor while I was there. I'm not talking about dust, Alex! I am talking about filth!'

'Please, don't be so hysterical. The dog only peed on the floor because it's a puppy. It's getting house trained,' I say with exaggerated patience.

'The whole place is a complete tip. There was a motorbike in the hallway!'

'Well, I don't care!' I shout with a sudden burst of temper. 'I like it there.'

'You are coming to Yorkshire.' My mother's voice is low and steely, more frightening in its way than my father's blustering. She shoots a look bordering on disgust at my father as she continues: 'Seth has organized everything. It's wonderful to have someone to take control.'

My father is looking down at the floor, his hands are still balled into fists but the fight has gone out of him.

'It's all been settled, so your father won't be expected to do anything at all, which is just as well.' She turns to him and continues, her tone silky: 'It's all worked out fine because Seth's daughter, Faye, is coming over from the States for the summer and she'll keep an eye on Alex. They'll be company for each other. Girls are so much more mature than boys. Seth says Faye's coped brilliantly with the divorce. And his ex is not the easiest person in the world to get on with, not by a long way.'

For a second my eyes connect with my father's. He gives me this strange look and for a moment I could almost feel sorry for him. But I'm too busy feeling sorry for myself.

My mother has really hurt my pride by assuming that I have become some kind of delinquent because my parents aren't living together any more. I imagine her and Seth McElroy swapping notes about their kids, and I feel almost delirious with rage at the thought of them talking about 'poor Alex' who isn't coping. Viciously, I wonder what the perfect Faye has done which shows her to be managing so well. And find, in that moment of irrational rage, that it is possible to hate someone who you have only just found out exists.

'Me getting suspended has got nothing to do with you two getting divorced!' I say angrily. 'You think everything in the world revolves around you two, don't you? I slammed Palmer one because he's always got on my nerves. He's a sarky smug bastard, and I'd had enough of it. He'd have got a smack off me one day anyway.'

'You've never been in trouble before, Alex. And please don't keep swearing,' my mother says sharply, shooting another evil look at my father, as if he is the sole cause of this sudden eruption of bad language.

'Maybe it isn't such a good idea for you to pack up

and leave for Yorkshire. It's very unsettling for Alex. He is in the middle of his A level course.' My father turns on my mother, his face red and angry.

'Well! It's OK for you to jump ship and do exactly what you want, isn't it? I don't remember you thinking much about Alex when you were rushing off getting that girl pregnant.' My mother is trembling with sudden temper. 'I deserve my bit of happiness too, you know,' she snaps.

'Jeez! Please! Cool it!' I shout at them. 'I don't particularly care where I go or what I do. I just don't want you two belly-aching about me. Fight about something else.'

This outburst silences them for a moment and they both turn to look at me. 'As I have no choice in the matter, and I have to go to Yorkshire, I'm going to start packing my things,' I say with dignity. Then I turn to my father. 'I suggest you go away and give us a bit of peace. Get Mandy to take you to a fatherhood class or something . . . You'll need it,' I add ominously.

Yorkshire is a dump. As soon as we arrive I start to plan how I can get away. For a start it's raining. Not a good downpour, when it rains for a bit and then stops, like it does sometimes when I visit my grandparents on the Isle of Wight. No . . . this is a grey gloomy rain, as if the sky has fallen in. A low persistent drizzle covers the trees in damp cobwebs of moisture. And when we get out of the car it hangs on our faces like a heavy dew and pearls my mother's golden hair with a million glistening droplets.

'It's a lovely house, darling,' my mother says to Seth, as we stand and gaze at the cottage. Her voice is a little bit too high, and I know she is looking at the creeper which smothers the house and thinking about all the spiders and earwigs that will be coming in through the windows.

Seth, oblivious to my mother's deeply phobic nature,

is going off like a geriatric boy scout: hooting with pleasure and rushing around; just because the place is a couple of hundred years old he is completely ecstatic.

'I can't wait to show you around. This place was a real find,' he gloats. 'We have an open fire in the sitting-room and a range in the kitchen. It's all absolutely authentic. We even chop our own logs. Come on, Alex,' he says enthusiastically to me. At any moment I expect him to break into a campfire song.

We make our way around the side of the house through a dripping garden. The air is sharp and smells of countryside: flowers, earth, and the pungent reek of animals. Seth opens the back door with a flourish. The lintel is so low Seth and I have to duck our heads as we enter. The door leads straight into a big gloomy kitchen, the floor is uneven stone flags and it smells damp and mushroomy. I shoot a glance at my mother's face—it looks like it has been dipped in concrete.

Hiding a smirk I listen as Seth points out the beams and inglenooks; but really I am watching my mother clocking the pot sink, the solid fuel cooker, and an ancient washing machine hidden like a dank toad behind a drooping curtain.

'Darling, it's wonderful. It has such atmosphere,' my mother says too enthusiastically. Seth can't know her very well, or he'd suss she's lying through her teeth. 'I'll just get my coat from the car. It's a little chilly in here.'

'Oh, don't worry, sweetheart, it's got central heating. There's an oil tank hidden in the bushes at the back. Mod cons but with all the original features too.' Seth's face is beaming.

When my mother has her coat on we go upstairs. I opt for the attic bedroom which has its own little staircase. There's no wardrobe, only a hook on the back of the door. The only other furniture is a narrow bed under a skylight window.

'The bedrooms *are* a bit primitive,' Seth admits

reluctantly. My mother is silent, struck dumb by the awfulness of the horsehair mattresses and creaking brass bedsteads. 'We'll go into town and buy some duvets and towels. I think that's all it needs,' he adds.

If it was my father who had rented this place for the summer my mother would be having a major stress and screaming at him that it needs gutting not bed linen. But she just smiles fondly at Seth, as one would a boisterous dog or lunatic.

'Yes,' she says. 'We'll get everything flowery and cottagy, to complement the house. A pretty Liberty print, or something very Laura Ashley.'

As they clatter down the stairs I hear her add: 'I just wonder, with Faye coming, if we can manage with that washing machine. There's no silk cycle and no tumble dryer.'

Seth is laughing and telling my mother there is a drying line in the garden. If I wasn't feeling so dejected and cold I could almost find it funny.

They don't ask me if I want to go into town. So I spend the afternoon lugging my books and suitcases up to the attic. Then I appropriate a few bits of furniture from the rest of the house: a wooden chest for my clothes, a bookcase, and a reading light. After that I lie down on the bed and look at the grey sky through the sloping window. Really I ought to be doing school work but I can't concentrate.

Eventually I get up and explore the kitchen. The fridge is very old and makes a strange whirring noise. I wonder if my mother realizes there is no freezer or microwave here. Whoever has rented us the cottage has left milk in the fridge. There is also a pantry with bread, cheese, eggs, and tomatoes on a white-tiled shelf.

I make myself a tomato sandwich but what I really want is a coffee, so I poke about with the stove. When I open the door I discover that newspaper, sticks, and lumps of coaly stuff have been left in a neat pyramid inside it.

There are matches on the shelf above, and when I light the paper it takes the flame immediately and a friendly orange glow appears. Soon the stove is roaring like a steam train and I am so pleased with myself that I go into the sitting-room and light the fire in there too.

The sitting-room looks out over the road and is full of cracked leather furniture. There isn't a fitted carpet, just grainy floorboards and a square rug, and it smells of damp, dust, and old things; but the fire cheers it up and fills the room with the aroma of wood smoke, a definite improvement on mildew. I begin to almost feel happy as the old-fashioned kettle begins to steam and I make myself strong black coffee.

When the phone starts to ring I don't remember where it is kept, and run around the kitchen for a moment, disorientated, then I locate it in a narrow hallway leading to the front door. Lifting the receiver of the old bakelite phone I reel off the number written on the dial.

'Hi! Is Seth there, please?' A long, slow feminine drawl that is much more Yankee than Seth's clipped mid-Atlantic tones.

'He's not here. You'll have to call back later,' I reply shortly. I don't know why I thought the call would be for me because no one knows this number, but even so a ridiculous feeling of disappointment fills me.

'When's he due back? And who is that speaking, please?' A haughty tone. 'I'm ringing from the States and I need to contact him urgently.'

'Well, he's not here. So it doesn't really matter where you're ringing from,' I retort quickly, just in case the caller thinks I'm impressed by the fact that she's phoning from America. 'And I haven't got a clue when he'll be back. Probably when the shops shut,' I add, thinking that my mother will be keeping him busy.

'Who is that, please?' I sense a note of desperation in the tone now. 'Who are you?'

'I'm Alex.'

'*Alex?*' Her voice says very clearly that she doesn't have a clue who the hell I am.

'I'm Diane's son,' I say, my face growing hot from humiliation.

'Alexander! I didn't know you'd be there,' the voice muses.

'Obviously not. Why don't you call back later?' I don't say the words, 'And stop wasting my time', but the message is implicit in my tone.

'How much later do you suggest?' she asks softly.

'I don't know.'

'Alexander. What time do the shops close there in England?' She is talking to me as if I am a small child.

'I don't know,' I say irritably. 'We're in Yorkshire now. They may not even have shops up here for all I know. And I don't particularly care. Some of us don't live to shop. It hasn't become an art form over here yet!'

There is a brief pause, as if the person on the other end has been rendered dumb by my blatant anti-American rudeness. And I feel a moment of triumph before the voice says quietly:

'Alexander, would you please give Seth a message. It's very important.'

'Yes, I can do that.'

'Would you tell him I've changed my plans and I will be arriving at the weekend. I'll ring later to confirm flight times, but I've arranged to fly into . . . ' I hear her shuffling papers and tickets at the other end of the phone. 'Into a place called Yeadon. If he could meet up with me, please, I'd be real grateful.'

'Yeeaidon,' I repeat, with unconscious mimicry. 'I'll tell him.'

'Thank you, Alexander. I sure appreciate your help,' she says, then the line goes dead, and I am left wondering if she was being sarcastic. I scribble a message for Seth and leave it by the phone.

Suddenly I am oppressed by the smoky darkness of the house, it's as if a dirty cloth is being wrapped around my face. I pull on my jacket and walk out leaving the back door unlocked. My mother's belongings are still locked in her car, and if anyone wants to hump my stuff down from the attic to steal they are welcome to it.

Slowly I wander down the road, under the dripping trees. At the bottom of the hill, where the road is wider, there are a few houses and a small Post Office. Rattling the change in my pocket, I go into the Post Office and buy a bar of fruit and nut.

'Could you tell me where the village is?' I ask the old woman behind the counter, as I unwrap the chocolate.

'What village might that be?' she replies with a smile. She doesn't have too many teeth. I turn away because I get the feeling she is laughing at me.

'Gouthgill?' I say cautiously.

'Well, this here's Gouthgill Post Office, and the church is down there,' she gestures with her thumb. 'And there's the houses in between.'

'Quite a metropolis . . . ' I break off a chunk of chocolate and cram it in my mouth.

'You're from Rose Cottage, aren't you? Staying with that actor chap?'

'Yes.'

'Well, if you like walking there's a grand walk around the lake. Go through the churchyard and out of back gate. It's a grand walk. You'll enjoy it.'

'Thanks,' I say gratefully. It seems so long since anyone cared what I did, or whether I enjoyed myself, that I set off as guileless as a lost dog.

The church is a shock. The windows are broken, boarded up in places. I walk slowly up the overgrown path, looking at the gravestones which lean into each other and are stained with livid lichens and mosses. The grass covering the grave humps is cropped short and marked in

31

places by round pellets of dung, a musky animal smell hangs in the damp air.

Sensing something behind me I turn quickly, and come face-to-face with a long, white, furry face topped by two horns. For a moment my mouth is dry with panic. Then I see a tethering rope, long legs, cloven hoofs, and know that the creature facing me is no ghastly vision of Satan, but merely a goat.

The creature moves nearer and snuffles fondly at my cuff. I back away from the sweaty stink of it: 'Clear off, get away from me!' I yell.

Turning, intending to walk quickly away, I am stopped by the glimpse of a slim grey-skirted figure disappearing around the side of the church. And I know that someone else, a girl, is in the churchyard and has witnessed my startled meeting with the goat. I feel a real prat.

I walk slowly, expecting to see whoever it is as I turn the corner. Finding that I am wishing for, and yet dreading, the expected meeting. Dreading seeing a knowing, supercilious smile; and yet glad, in the dripping forlornness of the graveyard, to have sight of another human face, however mocking or unkind.

But there is no one there. She must have sped away like a child. I stop at the rustic gate, overgrown with creepers and wild roses, and look back at the sightless, broken windows and dark arch of the church porch. With a shudder I wrench open the gate. The weeds are thick and I have to force it. Then I speed down the footpath as if pursued.

4

My desire to get away from the goat, the church, and the girl who doesn't want to talk to me, is so great that I walk about halfway around the lake before I know it.

Pausing to get my breath I look back at the water, which is coiled like a great grey snake along the base of the valley. Beech trees, over-laden with summer leaves, have turned the path into a deep tunnel, where great drops of water rain down on me like a shower of silver bullets.

The world is strangely noiseless: the only sound echoing through the mist is the plaintive call of water-birds and they sound as forlorn as lost children crying for their mothers. My trainers are absolutely soaked and I'm really depressed. All I can think about is the girl in the graveyard who ran away from me; and also about the other girl, Faye, from America, who called me Alexander. No one but my grandparents call me Alexander. That Yankee girl must be really snobby to call people by their full name like that. And I know that if we ever meet, I shan't like her.

Eventually I turn back and retrace my steps. When I get to the church the goat comes rushing to meet me, pulling at his rope. A lonely walk in the rain has mellowed my feelings towards him. When he pushes and nuzzles against my sodden jacket he seems like the only friend I will ever have.

In my jeans pocket I find the last square of chocolate and tentatively hold it out to him. He takes it very carefully from my nervously outstretched hand, his lips surprisingly soft against my finger tips.

'There you are, old fella. I'll bring you something else tomorrow,' I say genially. And as I leave the churchyard he strains at the tethering rope, looking after me with longing eyes.

My mother and Seth have returned from their shopping trip. The kitchen table is piled high with boxes and carrier bags. I shrug off my wet jacket and trainers. It's colder in the house than outside. If this is Yorkshire in the summer, I'd hate to be here in the winter.

The fire in the sitting-room has gone out, but the cooker in the kitchen is still alight. I heap more fuel on the glowing coals and huddle in the alcove next to the stove, drying my feet and trying to get warm.

My eyes grow heavy and I must have dozed right off, because the next thing I know the kitchen is dark and I can hear this weird noise and the sound of running water in the sink. My feet have been so close to the stove they feel on fire. It is with relief that I put them down on to the cold stone floor and lean forward.

The weird noise is Seth humming. He is filling a brand-new electric kettle with water and plugging it into a socket. Then he starts to unwrap parcels; a tea pot, china mugs, and a jug. I know I ought to say hello or something. I could say: 'If you're making tea I'll have a cup, please.' But no words will come and I sit in the alcove, tucked into the dark shadow, acting like I'm deaf and dumb.

Hanging my head, I try not to watch him padding around the kitchen, wishing I could also block the noise from my ears. Seth gives up with the humming and starts singing an aria from an opera—giving those Italian words a real trip around his lungs and sinuses before he spits them out. Normally I am not a praying kind of person, but I find I am asking God to please make him disappear. My feet have cooled down to ice again and I start to shiver. If it were possible I would transport myself back to the graveyard with the goat—it would seem like heaven compared to this.

Seth brings the tea pot over to the stove. Even though I don't move a muscle he spots me and lets out this great startled yelp. At the same time he drops the tea pot. It smashes on the floor into a zillion pieces.

'Jeezzus H. What the HELL?' he yells at me.

'Sorry . . . ' I say lamely. I can't look at him, my eyes keep sliding away from his bare legs and short towelling dressing gown. Instead I stare down at his slippers—they are navy blue towelling mules. I suppose he thinks he can get away with things like that, being an actor. I wouldn't be seen dead flip-flopping around the house like some half-baked housewife.

'Hell's bells, kid.' He leans against the stove and puts his hand to his chest. 'You scared the life out of me. What are you doing hiding in there?'

'I'm not hiding!' I say. 'I was just getting warm.'

'We thought you'd gone out for the evening,' he says. The shock has given way to annoyance now. 'Why didn't you shout to us when you came in? Instead of creeping around.'

'I wasn't bloody creeping around.' My voice is starting to rise and I can't stop it. 'Anyway, I am going out now.'

Up in my room I forage around in my suitcase for a jumper and some dry socks. When I get down to the kitchen my mother is sweeping up the broken china.

'I'm going to be fixing some supper soon,' she says, without looking up. 'So don't be long.' I don't answer, just go out and slam the door.

It's nearly dark outside. I've never been anywhere that didn't have street lights and houses. So this is the first time I have come up against the blackness of the night unpolluted by man and it makes me feel excited. At first I walk uncertainly, but by the time I get to the gate my eyes have grown accustomed to the soft velvety dusk.

Setting off down the hill I walk quickly to get warm. Inside my head is a jumble of thoughts: all about how I will go back to London as soon as I can; how I will hate Faye on sight; and how the country will drive me mad if I stay here for more than 48 hours.

Eventually I get to a main road. Away in the distance there are lights and I head for those—civilization is ahead! First I find a bus stop. It is too dark now to read the bus timetable fixed on the side of a small wooden shelter, but just the sight of a bus stop cheers me. I speculate on which town the bus will go to and what it will be like. Down hill from the bus stop is the village hall. It's made from corrugated iron and looks like something left over from the last war.

Ahead of me I can see a cluster of lights, flickering and winking. When I get close I find a long low building with window boxes full of dejected pansies and an illuminated sign: 'The Gamekeeper's Lodge'.

Jangling the money in my pocket I get a buzz of excitement. This feeling doesn't last too long, because as soon as I walk in through the door I realize that the pub is as authentically awful as everything else in Gouthgill: spit, sawdust, and OAP land. The door leads straight into one long bar room, with a bare wood floor and some faded old rugs. There are a few tables and chairs, a dart board, and an ancient juke-box playing crummy country songs from the 1970s. At a table in front of the open fire sit a couple of old men playing dominoes, apart from them the place is deserted.

As I walk across to the bar, ignoring the stares of the locals, I realize that most of my money is small change and I haven't got my wallet with me. There is no one behind the bar. The song on the juke-box whines to a stop and the place is suddenly silent, apart from the barking of a dog in the dark night outside.

'What do you have to do to get a drink around here?' I ask one of the old men. He doesn't answer me, just tilts his head back and shouts: 'Gracie!' A girl appears from the back regions. She is very young, with baby-fine blonde hair and rather goofy teeth, but she smiles at me welcomingly.

'Good evening,' I say, leaning on the bar. 'Could I have a half of bitter, please?' In normal circumstances I would ask her to have a drink with me, but I don't think I've got enough cash. She serves me, puts the money in the till, and then disappears again. I had hoped she would stop and talk. It isn't much fun standing by the bar alone and drinking the flat sour-tasting beer she has left me. Wandering over to the fire I watch the old men for a few minutes, but they are absorbed in their game and don't look up.

After that I drink the beer too quickly, because there is nothing else to do. When I have finished it I don't feel like shouting for Gracie. I try coughing and when that doesn't work I tap the bar top with my last pound coin. This time a man appears. He is short and barrel-shaped with a square bad-tempered face.

'Half of bitter, please, and a bag of crisps, cheese and onion.' It's humiliating to have to count out 5 pences for the beer and crisps.

'You can have that now you've paid for it. But next time you come into my pub you bring your ID.' The man narrows his eyes at me. Gracie has come back into the bar, standing in the doorway, chewing her thumb nail, watching me with a mixture of hostility and wonder.

'ID!' I take a gulp of the beer.

'Yes. Summat to prove you're eighteen or over.' The man sneers openly at me now and that really annoys me. Sense tells me to finish my beer and get out: but something, maybe Gracie's curious gaze, I don't know, makes me continue the conversation.

Leaning on the bar, as if the landlord and I are mates, I say with an affability I don't feel. 'To tell you the truth— I've stopped carrying ID since I had my twenty-first birthday.'

'And the bloody rest,' the landlord adds cryptically. 'I

don't want no smart answers from the likes of you. You want to drink in here—I want to see your ID.'

I drink the beer down in one go and wipe my mouth with the back of my hand. 'I don't think I'll bother. Your beer's pretty foul!' I say over my shoulder, as I make for the door. From behind me I hear Gracie begin to titter nervously.

Once outside I realize that a pint of beer guzzled down too quickly on an empty stomach has made me feel dizzy and a bit sick. I also realize that nothing in the world is going to keep me in this godforsaken place—I'll go back to London tomorrow.

When I wake up in the morning I find a square of brilliant blue above my head. For a moment I can't quite work out where I am or what this wonderful slab of colour is. Then I realize it is the sky, framed by the sloping window of my attic room. I lie back and study the flawless colour above me: thinking about the words we use to describe shades of blue and skies, and finding that nothing comes close to summing up the wonderful sight of that hot, bright blueness above my head.

Jumping up, I open the skylight wide so I can poke my head through. A miracle has happened: the rain and greyness have disappeared and in their place is a world miraculously new-washed and fragrant. Yorkshire, or at least this small hidden corner, is beautiful. Down in the valley the lake shimmers like an exotic serpent, and the trees move gracefully in the breeze like milkmaids in billowing green gowns.

Gulping down lungfuls of the air I find that it's sweet and sharp, like chilled wine or ice-cream, and it makes me want to laugh and shout—suddenly it's good to be alive. I shelve any plans to go back to London today. This sunshine is too good to miss.

Into my head come snippets of poetry. I'd never really

got into Wordsworth and the other Romantics, but now it's as if a missing piece of jigsaw puzzle has suddenly fallen into place. Now I understand why they were excited by nature and the countryside, because this day, this blueness, this sharp intensity of the senses, has made me feel quite intoxicated.

I creep down the narrow stairs, listening hard. The cottage is not silent, it creaks and sighs, but there are no sounds of people. Tip-toeing into the kitchen I find a note on the table. *Alex, we will be back this evening. Salad for lunch in fridge. Mum.*

Childishly I want to prance and dance around the kitchen and whoop out loud. They have gone and left me and I have this last beautiful day all to myself. I arrange an enormous breakfast of cornflakes and toast on a tray and take it outside. There I sit with the sun in my face, listening to the sound of bird song.

After I have showered and dressed I get all the bread from the bread bin and go down to the church. Three goats appear from behind the gravestones as soon as I arrive, pulling at their ropes to get across to me.

There is the white goat, my friend from yesterday, whom I call Snowy; a piebald creature with strange amber eyes; and a brown goat with ugly broken ears, whom I immediately nickname Droopy. They nearly knock me over trying to eat the bread from my hands and poke their noses into all my pockets. I would never have guessed that goats have gentle mouths and are dainty eaters, they nibble at my fingers as if they are kissing me. It's fun giving them pieces of bread and telling them off for pushing.

'They're all nannies . . . ' says a voice from behind me and I spin around as if shot. 'So you mustn't say "bad boy" to them.' The voice has laughter in it. It's the girl from yesterday, of that I'm sure. She's dressed in dirty jeans and a ragged man's shirt which nearly reaches her knees, by her side is a scrawny dog with long legs and an enormous head.

'Are they yours?' I ask. She moves forward and the dog comes too, it isn't on a lead but keeps next to her as if joined by an invisible rope. I had assumed she was a little girl because she's so small, but when she's standing next to me I realize that there are definite curves beneath the shirt and she might easily be my age. And just for a moment I wish I'd combed my hair or put on some of Seth's aftershave.

'Yes, they're mine,' she says cheerfully, she reaches out and the goats move forward to nuzzle her hands.

'I've been giving them some bread.'

'I know. I've been watching you for ages,' she says, and my face goes hot because I've been talking absolute rubbish to those goats.

'You talk to them, that's really nice,' the girl says, grinning at me, amused by my discomfort. 'They like that, don't you, my old darling?' As she says this, she reaches down and kisses Snowy's nose. This makes me laugh out loud and I don't feel quite so foolish any more.

Hard though I try, I cannot stop staring at the girl. She doesn't look like anyone I have ever met before. Her long browny-blonde hair is coiled in dreadlocks and she has a very tanned freckled face. Her hands, which are stroking the goats, are square and tough, like small brown claws, not like a girl's hand at all. When she turns to look at me her bright blue eyes have a slight squint and are coolly calculating: she reminds me of a Siamese cat.

With an effort I drag my gaze away. There is something raw and real about her that makes me glad now I hadn't bothered with aftershave. The cuffs of her cotton shirt are frayed and her jeans look as if someone wore them out long before she got them. Her big boots are as scuffed and faded as a workman's. Also she is very grubby—and it's not designer dirt and hair gel like we have in London—it's the real thing.

I peer at her again. The skin on her face is tightly etched across the bones, so that already there are little laughter lines around her eyes and a groove from her nose to the corner of her mouth.

'Do you live around here?' I ask, thinking she might be from a travelling family.

'Yeah,' she gestures with her thumb. 'Cottage down by the lakeside. My da works on the estate.'

'Oh? Is there an estate?' I prompt her.

She nods. 'If you go up to top of road you'll see a big wall. It goes right round the castle and grounds. Sir Thomas Crossley and his family live in there. They own all the land and farms around here. Rich like you wouldn't believe.' She narrows her eyes and stares at me. 'You into blood sports?'

This really throws me. I wonder if it is some kind of trick question. It takes me a moment to work out what she is talking about.

'Blood sports?' I find myself echoing idiotically. 'Leave it out! I'm from London.'

She bursts out laughing at this: 'You anti then?'

'Yes!' I say quickly. To be honest, blood sports are not something I'd really thought about before. I mean, we'd debated the topic at school, but it never really meant anything to me. Now I find it matters. 'I really hate the idea of killing animals for fun,' I add, in what I hope is a suitably serious voice.

The girl looks at me slyly and smiles, a small secret smile. 'Good,' she says with satisfaction. 'I'm Louie, by the way.'

'I'm Alex,' I say, grinning at her.

'I heard you'd been in the pub. Giving old Barnes a bit of lip.'

'Who did you hear that from?' I enquire.

'Gracie told me.'

'Really?' I'm ridiculously flattered that my rudeness has been repeated.

'I saw her this morning. She was going for the school bus.'

41

'Don't you go to school?'

Louie grins at me, she has very small, rather sharp, teeth and she looks more like a cat than ever when she smiles. 'Only when I have to and I've been once this week.'

'Haven't you got exams and important things like that?' I am curious about her age.

'Oh—we've done them,' she says carelessly. 'I've got too much to do to hang around school doing sports and boring stuff like that.' She moves away from me suddenly, shifting restlessly, as if she's keen to be off.

'What kind of things?' I ask, trying to keep the conversation going. I'm enjoying talking to her. And I am desperate not to be relegated to 'boring stuff' along with school and society in general.

She shrugs. 'I've got animals. You still at school or working?'

'I'm still at school. A levels next year.' Louie looks remarkably unimpressed by this so I add quickly: 'I've been suspended—that's why I'm here.'

Louie smiles broadly. That has impressed her. 'Suspended . . . ' she rolls the word around her mouth. 'What for?'

'I hit someone . . . ' I say nonchalantly, as if this was something I did every day.

'That the truth?' Louie obviously doesn't think I look the right type for physical violence. It seems pointless to lie to her. I get the feeling she would see right through me.

'Yeah. But I don't make a habit of it,' I add truthfully.

'Do you like animals?' She is slowly shifting away from me, moving like a wild animal herself: stealthily, with a minimum of movement, and the dog is following her like a shadow.

'Yes. Yes I do. We don't have any pets, but I like animals.' I move with her and hold out my hand to her dog. 'I like your dog, what's he called?'

'Don't touch him,' she says warningly. 'He doesn't like strangers.' I pull my hand back quickly.

'He's called Blue. He's a lurcher. He's a grand dog. I've got to go now.' She moves right away then, but I fall into step with her.

'Where are you going?' Even though I tower above her, and am undoubtedly older, I feel like a little kid following a bigger kid around hoping to be included in their game.

'To see my horse.' She gives me a sideways look, weighing me up. Then she adds: 'You can come if you want.'

'OK,' I say.

Louie leads me through the graveyard and down to the side of the lake. We cut through a wood and down a cart track. At the end of the lane there is a cottage which has a sagging slate roof and smoke rising from the chimney in a blue plume. When we finally emerge into a field I realize we are now behind the cottage and can look up into a garden, where a line of greyish sheets are flapping in the sunshine and small children are playing.

At the top of the field are lots of small huts built from odd bits of timber and old sheets of corrugated iron; they are connected by ramshackle fences and bits of chicken wire. It reminds me of a shanty town.

Louie sees me staring and says: 'I built all that myself. It's where I keep my animals. Here's Fred . . . ' A huge horse has heard her voice and is loping across the field towards us. I am petrified, but try not to show it. I've never been in a field with a horse before and the sheer size is overpowering. The horse is blowing through its nose and nuzzling at Louie. I stand very still and hope it won't come any closer to me.

'It's all right. He won't hurt you,' Louie says, and I detect a note of amused contempt in her voice.

'Do you . . . do you ride him?' I ask, trying to swallow my fear.

Louie laughs as she produces a carrot from her pocket and gives it to the horse.

'No one rides Fred any more. He's past his sell-by-date; broken winded, lame in two legs, sway backed. He was on his way to the knacker's yard when I got him. So now he's here for a well-earned rest . . . aren't you, my old boy?'

She rests her head against the horse's neck in a moment of pure unashamed devotion. The horse whinnies as if in answer. I am totally and utterly mesmerized by Louie and Fred. It's like a scene from *Black Beauty*.

'I have to keep him alive on oats and pony nuts soaked in hot water . . . ' she confides. 'He's had a lifetime of work—but now he's going out in style with the best of everything.'

'Must cost you a fortune,' I say, more to make conversation than anything else. But Louie gives me a very odd look, her blue eyes suddenly like arctic ice.

'I've got work to do. See you later, maybe,' she says abruptly. She strides off up the hill towards the huts with Fred and Blue following her. I have been frozen out. To be honest, I get the feeling Louie would like me more if I had four legs.

'Can I bring Fred some carrots?' I call after her rather desperately.

She turns and grins. 'Yeah, if you want to. He likes apples as well.'

'What about the goats?' I ask, despising myself for being so ingratiating and so desperate for the girl's goodwill.

'They'll eat anything. If they come into your garden watch your washing . . . ' she laughs, but not unkindly. 'I'll be seeing you,' she adds, and then she is gone.

Despondently I make my way back to the house, walking slowly. The day has clouded over and so has my mood. Everyone but me is busy. Everyone has something important to do with their life. Whereas all I have is a heap of school work or the prospect of packing up my stuff. Neither of these holds any appeal at the moment.

My mind is so full of these thoughts that I get to the gate of the cottage before I realize that there is someone sitting on the front doorstep among a pile of luggage. When I open the gate the figure jumps up. I stand, frowning, surveying the mound of bags, the huge suitcases, vanity boxes, and duty-free plastic carrier bags.

'You're travelling light, I see?' I say at last.

A small dark-haired girl holds out her hand to me. 'Hi, you must be Alexander. I'm Faye. Am I glad to see you! I thought I might be sitting here till evening time.'

'You said the weekend. No one is expecting you.'

'It was so lucky—I got a standby flight. I did try to phone. In the end I just grabbed a cab and hoped for the best.' She smiles a radiant grin at me. 'And it's all turned out OK, because here you are!'

'Well, you better come in . . . ' I say ungraciously as I begin to lift the largest of the bags.

'I was worried it was going to rain . . . ' she says, lifting the smaller bags.

'Humph . . . ' is all I reply. I pretend that I am concentrating on the luggage, but in fact I am trying not to stare at her. She is, without doubt, the most beautiful girl I have ever seen. But this realization doesn't fill me with joy. Instead, a feeling of sick apprehension and deep gloom engulfs me, because this is Faye, the girl I am going to hate.

5

My mother goes crackers over Faye—just like I knew she would. I have spent the whole afternoon carrying bags upstairs and making the wretched girl cups of coffee but I am brushed aside: 'Alex! Have you looked after Faye?' is all my mother says, and then it's one long sucking-up session.

My mother hugs Faye and then, still holding on to her shoulders, stands back and says almost tearfully: 'Why, you're more beautiful than your photos. We're so pleased to see you.' Any minute I expect my mother to start kissing her or something really embarrassing.

Anyway, she contents herself with showing Faye all these special wonderful things she's bought because Faye is coming to stay: a water filter, a coffee machine, extra thick duvets, a mirror and electric toothbrush for the bathroom . . . Let's hope and pray Faye and my mother never get shipwrecked on a desert island together—they wouldn't last two days without mod cons.

'There's just one problem, Diane. I can hardly get into my room now because of the suitcases. Do we have a garage or a basement where I could store them?'

'Well, there's only the attic and Alex is sleeping up there,' my mother says doubtfully.

'I couldn't inconvenience Alexander—he's been wonderful—carrying all my heavy bags for me.' Faye gives me this glittering smile: her teeth flashing like a sudden glimpse of snow. When I scowl in reply she and my mother share a conspiratorial smile together. And I lumber out of the room, like some half-trained performing bear, knowing that when I am safely out of earshot my mother will say: 'Boys of his age are so difficult . . . ' or something like that, and she and Faye will laugh together.

Retreating to my room I attempt to do some work. I am reading Hardy's *Jude the Obscure* and it's really depressing. The other really depressing thing is that it has started raining. It seems impossible after the glorious morning and I'm sure the weather doesn't do bizarre things like this in London. Up in my attic the downpour sounds like a monstrous regiment marching across the slates, and the skylight is filmy with grey streaky rain. Eventually I get under the duvet and try to read, but the words keep bobbing around, because my thoughts are full of Faye.

She is exactly six months older than me, I know because she told me, after asking me how old I am. So she is seventeen . . . She might as well be seventy-seven the gulf between us is so wide. My mind keeps going back to her, like a dog worrying at a bone, as I try to work out why she is so much more grown-up than I am. Is it because she is American?—a precocious brat? Partly. But it's not just that. I think back to my first sight of her. First impressions are very important. When you first see Faye you don't think—here's a girl, but—here is a small woman. Her hair is cut so it swings around her face and she wears jewellery, not nose studs and earrings and the junky stuff the girls at school wear, but proper jewellery: pearl and diamond droplets in her ears, which peep out when her hair moves, and gold chains, one around her neck and one around her ankle. Her skin is smooth and clear and she wears red lipstick. But it isn't just those things which make her grown-up: it is the cool appraisal in her dark eyes when she looks at you, the careful way she speaks, her ability to say the right thing at the right time.

'Little Miss Perfect . . . ' I mutter angrily to myself.

By the time supper is ready I'm in a really bad mood. We sit around the kitchen table and my mother lights some candles. She's put out heavy red napkins and wine glasses in Faye's honour.

'We'll start with soup and crusty bread,' my mother says. 'Then I've rustled up pasta and a green salad. Just a quick supper. It's difficult working full time and being a housewife.' Her face is so pious you would think getting supper on the table was a New Testament miracle or something.

'We'll take it in turns, that will be fairer,' Faye says quickly. 'Do you like cooking, Alexander? If you don't, I could teach you.' She puts her head on one side and gives me a smile that would melt the polar ice cap. I hate being patronized and open my mouth to tell her so, but my mother butts in first.

'Alex is very good with frozen pizzas . . . ' she says, as if this is a very witty remark. There is laughter from the others. 'I'm sure there's lots you could teach him, Faye. That would be nice, wouldn't it, Alex?'

As she is speaking she is opening the bread bin. A little squeak comes out of her mouth: 'What's happened to all the bread? There was garlic bread, wholemeal rolls, and a crusty loaf in here this morning. Alex! Surely you haven't eaten it all? What on earth were you thinking of? There's nothing to have with the soup . . . ' Her voice is rising. The perfect mother is giving way to the shrew. Seth is staring at her in disbelief.

'Growing boys do get hungry . . . ' he says in a conciliatory tone. 'Did you have a triple-decker sandwich?' he asks me with a grin.

I stare back at him blankly. The atmosphere is thick with reproach and tension.

'Really, Alex! I think you do these things on purpose . . . ' my mother snaps. 'There is no freezer in this house . . . ' She is on the verge of getting upset and I wonder how long it will take Seth to realize she hates this cottage.

'Hey! Why don't we have crackers? I love biscuits and soup,' Faye says brightly. Little Miss Perfect has become Little Miss Peacemaker. Pukey! My mother produces Ryvita and we eat in silence.

My mother dishes up the pasta. Then she turns to Faye and asks, as if they are old friends: 'I thought Erik was going to come with you? Will he be coming later in the summer? We are looking forward to meeting him, aren't we, darling?' She and Seth share a smile. Seth nods his approval as he says to Faye:

'Your mom tells me that things are getting pretty serious between you and Erik.'

My mother has this soppy look on her face, like she's watching *The Sound of Music*. Seth is looking pretty misty-eyed as well, as if he's imagining himself walking Faye up the aisle.

My eyes move to Faye's face and I see her expression change. It's like watching a big cloud move across the sun. She moves her salad around on the plate and doesn't answer for a moment. Eventually, when the silence has grown unbearable, she mutters miserably: 'Erik won't be coming.'

'Not coming?' My mother echoes. She never knows when to keep quiet. You'd need a skin like a rhino not to see that Faye doesn't want to talk about it, but still my mother rushes on: 'That is a pity. Have you two fallen out?'

'I sure hope not,' Seth says menacingly. 'I thought he'd given you a ring and it was all . . . '

'Pop!' Faye lifts her head and her brown eyes are full of tears. 'I don't want to talk about it, not here, not now, not ever. Erik and I are completely over . . . finished . . . kaput. And talking about it isn't going to help.'

'It's just a lover's tiff . . . I'm sure you'll soon make up,' my mother says brightly. 'Is that why you came over early? He'll be pining for you by now,' she adds with a laugh.

'No he won't. And I cut school early because I've been ill,' Faye says, and there is something cold and steely in her voice which makes me stare at her. My mother begins to talk to Seth about work, but I sit and watch Faye. Her head droops forward like a flower on a broken stem and her hair falls like two dark curtains to hide her face. Then I see tears roll, like two small pearls, on to the pine tabletop. For some reason the sight of those tiny gleaming droplets makes me feel really sad.

'Have you got a girlfriend you want to invite up to visit during the vacation?' Seth turns and asks me. I jump, startled.

'Me?'

'Yes, you, buddy! Big, fine, handsome guy like you.' Seth grins, and I wonder if he is sending me up. But he says very sincerely to my mother, as if it's some kind of a compliment to her: 'I bet Alexander has the girls queuing to date him.'

Just for a moment Faye looks up and our eyes meet, hers full of some primitive hurt which I can't recognize.

'I have a headache,' she says quickly, before I can speak. 'I think it must be jet lag catching up with me. Would you excuse me, please? I don't think I want any more to eat . . . ' Rising to her feet she looks down at her plate of untouched food. 'I'm sorry. It really was very good.'

'Would you like a coffee?' my mother asks solicitously.

'No, thank you, Diane. I think I'll go to bed. Goodnight.'

Her early exit puts a real damper on the meal. My mother is icy with me—as if having no bread has been the cause of all the trouble. I eat all my pasta and the plate which Faye left. It makes me feel better to eat her dinner: as if I am a stray dog who has sneaked into the kitchen and eaten the supper of some pampered pet.

'I'm surprised you can eat anything at all after gorging all that bread!' my mother says crossly. Then I eat a whole family-sized dish of tiramisu, even though I am full, just to annoy her.

After that pig-out I go upstairs and lie down on my bed. My mother and Seth leave for the pub, I hear them talking as they shut the back door, Seth's foghorn voice disrupting the quiet of the twilight. When they have gone I listen to the sound of a bird singing deep in the thicket of the garden and wonder if it's a nightingale. Then I get Hardy's *Jude* out from under my pillow and find it isn't such hard work on a full stomach.

My concentration is broken by a disturbing choking noise seeping into my consciousness. At first I try to ignore it, but eventually I put my book down and lean out of the skylight window. Then I open my door and listen hard. The noise is coming from the bedroom below mine. Faye's room. She is crying. Not a noisy hysterical weeping, but a low quiet sobbing like the wind keening on a stormy night.

Irrational anger wells up inside me. I feel like going downstairs, opening her bedroom door, and shouting at her to shut up howling. It's just typical that little Miss Perfect should be suffering from a broken heart! I mean, the wretched girl has everything. I'd like the chance to have a broken heart, or even one that was a bit dented . . .

Turning on my ghetto blaster really loudly I stamp around on the floor hoping she can hear me, although I suppose she is too busy thinking about Erik to notice.

It's impossible to return to my book. I begin to imagine what will happen when Erik finds out she has fled to England to nurse her uncontrollable grief. He will, of course, follow her: which is probably what she wanted in the first place—proof of his undying devotion. So Erik will arrive at the first opportunity, maybe even in the morning. He will have travelled non stop, in just the clothes he stands up in, faded jeans and a lumberjack shirt. He will arrive with shadows under his eyes and the gleam of golden stubble on his cheeks, having travelled here straight from London. I see him striding down the road past the lake, tall and blond, a Viking king type. Faye will run down to the gate to meet him and it'll be like *Romeo and Juliet* or the couple in *Titanic*: star-crossed lovers, passionate kisses, and tears of joy.

Envy grips my guts. I start to really wish there was some girl in London crying her eyes out over me and not being able to eat her supper. Her parents asking in anxious whispers: 'Do you think she's becoming anorexic? She's hardly eaten since Alexander Harling was suspended and left London.'

There is no one, not even Teresa Crispin, who I had a bit of a fling with in the fourth year, who is going to be missing me. In retrospect I realize that I should have stuck with Teresa and waited to see if that little seed of liking between us could have grown into a big strong tree of lust. Instead I stopped taking her to the cinema because I got a place in the footie team and had to spend Saturday afternoons practising. At fourteen I thought Teresa was just the start of my love life: I didn't realize she was going to be my one and only chance.

Eleven A*s at GCSE, playing the saxophone and too much sport has really retarded me. Since Teresa I haven't even taken a girl out. Danny and I don't bother to get into boasting competitions at school. Danny says most of the blokes make it all up. Since my other mate, Jean-Paul, left our school Danny and I have got a bit of a routine: footie practice, swimming, snooker. And if we go to the cinema we go together; I suppose we are in a bit of a rut. Jeez! When I think about it we're like some old married couple!

It's all my mother's fault—she should have let me leave school and go to sixth form college. How are Danny and I meant to fancy girls we have been at school with since we were eleven? Not that Jean-Paul seems to have fared any better at his private college. The trouble is girls our age are all into older blokes with jobs and cars.

Last year I got quite attracted to Karin Sharpe who's in my English group. She's got really short red hair and a big wide mouth. One day I just looked at her and thought how attractive she was when she smiled. I did try to move things on a bit. Telling her that her essay on the Brontë sisters was very good, that sort of thing. But all that happened was she lent me some old book about Victorian women, which her mother had bought at a jumble sale, and told me it would help me get the Brontës' struggle for emancipation into perspective. Not exactly the start of a great love affair.

Anyway, what if the girls talk in the cloakroom like the boys do? Do I really want Karin Sharpe and the rest of the lower sixth talking about how experienced I am and what kind of kissing I'm good at? I think back to all the trouble Jean-Paul had when he dated a girl in our sixth form and the answer is a resounding NO.

Still, maybe Karin Sharpe is really missing me now I'm not at school. I console myself with a scenario of her saying how boring English tutorials are without me. 'All the sparkle has gone out of my life since Alex was sent away . . . ' that sort of thing. Eventually I get into bed and listen to the silence outside until sleep overtakes me.

It's dull in the morning; my window is full of soft whiteness. There are great coiling banks of fog rolling in over the lake, and the trees are draped in lacy veils of mist like ghostly brides.

I stay in bed until I hear Seth and my mother leave for work. Then I slip down to the kitchen. Of course, the wonderful Faye is already down there, cleaning up the kitchen with Domestos multiwipe and attacking the stove, which is spitting and hissing in protest like a scalded cat. Cereal, a jug of milk, and a bowl and mug have been left on the table for me.

'It smells like a swimming pool in here. Do you have a cleanliness fetish?' I ask rather wearily.

'I'm sorry, Alexander, I didn't think. Of course you

don't want me doing all this stuff while you're eating breakfast.' She pours coffee for us both and joins me at the table. Stuffing cornflakes into my mouth I pretend to read the box, but really I'm looking at her: she's wearing a baggy cotton T-shirt and leggings which end just below her knees and the skin on her arms and legs is smooth and golden. Today her hair is pulled back into a ponytail and she isn't wearing any make-up or earrings: I can just see the tiny holes in the lobes of her ears.

'I thought, after I've done the chores, I might get the bus into Barrowgate and do some shopping. Want to come, Alexander?' she asks kindly. 'We could look around and find a pub for lunch. Seth has told me lots about Yorkshire pub lunches, I can't wait to try one. What do you think?'

Staring down at my empty bowl I swallow my last mouthful. 'I'm meeting someone,' I say, without looking at her.

'OK,' she says, with an attempt at cheerfulness. 'Maybe some other time. Have you found people in the village friendly?'

'Yes! You'll love them! Try the local pub. The landlord is a charmer. You'll be able to write home about it.'

There's a puzzled expression on her face, a small frown shadowing her eyes.

'Alexander, tell me. Why do you dislike me so much?' she questions.

I hate the fact that I have made my feelings so obvious. My smile is tight and insincere as I say: 'Please don't take it personally, Faye. I don't like anyone very much at the moment.'

She shrugs and doesn't reply. Going into the pantry I start to fill my pockets with all the available carrots and apples.

'Can I get you anything in Barrowgate?' Faye asks. She has followed me across the kitchen and is watching me from the doorway. 'Some fruit, maybe?'

I give her a dark look. 'Thanks,' I mutter.

'You have some strange eating habits, Alexander,' she says with a trace of mockery, but her smile is kind, almost indulgent.

Without replying I walk out and leave her. As I march down the path I hear her voice floating behind me, carrying through the mist. 'Have a nice day, Alexander.'

'Eff off!' I mutter, and for some reason that makes me feel loads better, as if I have really got one over on her.

There are no goats in the graveyard, so I walk down the lane and through the wood to try to find Louie, hoping this isn't one of the days she has decided to go to school. Eventually I spot her in the field with Fred, picking things out of his old hooves and talking to him.

'Hello!' I say, hoping she will be pleased to see me. 'I brought him some carrots.' Like a conjurer I pull one out of my pocket and hold it out to him.

'Hang on a sec,' Louie says roughly. 'He'll have your thumb off if you feed him like that. He may be old but he's still got teeth that could bite a brick in half.' I take a hasty step backwards and Louie laughs, but not unkindly. 'Haven't you ever fed a horse before?'

'No,' I say honestly. 'I'm a poor deprived inner-city delinquent.'

Louie shows me how to make my hand flat like a plate and I give Fred a couple of carrots, hoping all the time she won't notice how my hand is shaking. 'Do you want to come and see the little 'uns?' she asks. 'I'm just about to give them a feed.'

As we make our way up the field Fred walks behind us, and every so often he nudges my back with his nose. I'm totally terrified and scuttle into the shelter of the first hut with relief.

'I got a full house at the moment,' Louie says, with a mixture of weariness and pride. She leads me over to a small run made from odd bits of wood. 'I just cleaned them out, but they're squitting everywhere. In one end and out the other,' she adds lovingly.

Leaning into the run she scoops out a small puppy and places it in my hands. I make a cradle in the crook of my arm and the puppy curls up against my chest. It's black and white with bluish eyes and a tail like a question mark.

'They got left in a bin bag. There were six, but one died.'

'Did you find them?' I ask wonderingly.

'No, people bring them to me. I've got a litter of kittens too. They got left at the gate in a box. People know I'll look after them. Sometimes the decent ones knock on the door and leave money for food and things.'

'But they're so tiny. How do they manage without a mother?'

Louie grins. 'I'm the only one they'll ever have. I fed 'em every two hours to begin with.'

'All through the night?' I ask, staggered.

'No. They can go for a bit longer at night unless they're very weak. I give them all a good feed at about midnight, have a bit of a kip and then start again at five. But they're nearly weaned now.' While she is talking, she is putting food into bowls and giving it to the puppies. The smell and sound of a meal being served makes my puppy wriggle and I have to put him down.

'I'm not surprised you don't have time to go to school,' I say, staggered by her mothering skills.

'School's boring.'

'Do you go to school in Barrowgate? What's it like?'

Louie shakes her head. 'I go in the other direction—to Yarham. Barrowgate's all right. I've got to go there today. Got to pick up some worming powder for this lot from the vet.'

'Going on the bus?'

She shakes her head. 'Costs a quid on the bus. I'm biking. Want to come?'

'I haven't got a bike,' I say regretfully.

'I could lend you our Jim's, if you want,' Louie says casually.

'Yeah, great,' I say with a grin. My smile becomes a little fixed when I see Jim's bike. For a start it's a lady's bike, so rusted and battered that it's impossible to say what colour it was originally, and the mudguard at the back is held on with dirty string.

As if reading my mind Louie says rather defensively, 'The brakes are fine. If you want to use it.' As her bike is even older and more decrepit I manage a smile and get on gingerly. After my mountain bike it's really heavy. I could well have a heart attack if there are many hills between here and Barrowgate.

The mist is beginning to thin and a soft hazy sunlight bathes the valley as we cycle slowly around the lake.

'Going to be hot later,' Louie says, dismounting at the foot of a hill. We stop for a moment to catch our breath and Blue disappears down to the lakeside for a drink.

'Does Blue go everywhere with you?'

'Yes. I have to tie him up when I go to school or he'd try to come too. He was dead jealous in the spring cos I got given five orphan lambs and I hand reared them. They thought I was their mam and followed me everywhere. Blue—he hated it.'

'What did you do with them?' I ask breathlessly, as we push the bikes up the hill.

'Sold them at the market. Get a good price for fat lambs.'

'I see . . . ' I say, rather shocked.

'Well, there's only two things you can make with a sheep, one's a woolly jumper, the other's a good stew. Anyway, I have to sell what I can to make enough money to keep the other animals.'

'Didn't you get fond of them?'

'Yeah, 'course I did. But you can't keep animals like that for pets.' Louie looks at me kindly. 'Biggest mistake I ever made was when I started keeping pigs. Called my first one Lawrence. Cried like a baby when the pig man came to do him. Since then they only have a number. You don't love 'em so much when they're called Pig Five.' She laughs ruefully.

'But why do you go on keeping them?' I say, swallowing hard.

'They eat all the old potatoes and scraps. Nothing's wasted with a pig. And face it, Alex, there's nothing like a bacon sarnie on a cold winter's morning, is there?' Louie says rather grimly.

We cycle on in silence, while I muse on life and death and bacon sandwiches.

Barrowgate is very small and old-fashioned. It has a market square with stocks and a Celtic cross marker. Apart from the cars parked nose to tail it could be lifted straight from a Hardy novel. As a concession to the traffic Louie puts a piece of orange twine around Blue's neck to make a halter.

Louie visits the vet's surgery and then we wander around the square. 'Shall we get some chips for lunch?' I ask; there is a divine smell coming from the chippy and I'm starving.

Outside the chip shop Louie gets out her purse. It's the kind of cheap thing a little kid has, red leather with a cartoon character on the side. Just seeing it makes me feel really sad for some reason, and when she peers inside and starts counting out her money, her lips moving in silent concentration, I feel awful.

'Ah, put it away, Louie. I'm standing lunch.'

'No, it's all right, I've got enough for some chips . . . '

'Look, I said I'm getting lunch,' I repeat. 'You lent me the bike. I'm treating you.'

'Ta then. I'll have chips and scraps.'

Once inside the shop I get a twenty pound note from my wallet and buy us everything I can think of. The woman has to put it in a carrier bag there's so much.

'Gordon Bennett!' Louie says, rolling her eyes, when I emerge triumphantly. 'You've got enough for an army.'

We cross the road and settle ourselves down on the steps of the market cross and I hand out parcels to Louie. Blue sits and watches us, dribble hanging from his mouth.

'I got us plaice, extra large. Thought we could do with a treat. Also on the menu today is chips, mushy peas, a bread roll, and a pickled egg. And here's a piece of chicken for Blue.'

Louie laughs. 'Thanks, Alex,' she says. Then she begins to set the food out on the paper, pushing chips into her mouth as she does so. When I see it spread out I realize that I have bought an awful lot and very much doubt I will be able to eat it all. To my amazement Louie eats every scrap of hers, right down to the last mushy pea. Then she tears the chicken into pieces and feeds it to Blue. As well as that I give him my pickled egg and half my plaice—he looks like the happiest dog alive.

Just as I am filling the carrier bag with the waste paper I hear my name. Looking up, squinting into the sun, I find Faye standing in front of me. She is dressed very neatly in a matching blue cotton shirt and trousers, with her hair tied up on top of her head. The dangly earrings are back in her ears and she is wearing pink lipstick. She looks totally grown-up and at ease. I, on the other hand, am conscious of my damp, sweat-soaked T-shirt and my greasy hands.

Wiping my mouth with my fingers I mutter: 'Hello.'

There is a long pause. I'm aware of Louie's puzzled stare, and I suddenly realize that it looks bad if I don't introduce her, so I add: 'This is Louie.'

'Hi, I'm Faye. I like your dog.'

Louie doesn't reply. As if appalled by our lack of human manners, Blue moves across and snuffles at Faye's hand as if they are old friends.

'Don't touch him. He doesn't like strangers,' I warn.

Blue, as if to show me to be a liar, then leans against Faye's legs, his plume of a tail beating out a tattoo of welcome.

'Faye just arrived from America yesterday,' I explain to Louie.

'Ah! You're staying at Rose Cottage too!' Louie says. 'I heard about you.' Again there is silence. Then Louie says to me: 'Is she your sister?'

Faye and I both say 'NO!' together, our voices in absolute union. We stare at each other as if dumb-struck by this.

'We're not related. Our parents are friends,' Faye explains politely, her brown eyes sliding away from mine.

Louie seems to have lost interest in us. She is getting hold of Blue's lead. 'I've got to get back. The kittens will need feeding soon,' she says to no one in particular.

'You have kittens, how lovely,' Faye says. 'I love cats,' she adds rather wistfully.

'Do you?' Louie asks, giving Faye one of her calculating sideways looks. 'Come up and see them then, they're grand at the moment. Maybe you'll want one. They'll need homes in a few days,' she adds, with a sly smile.

'OK. Thank you. I'll do that. I'd love to see them,' Faye says sincerely. 'It's been nice to meet you, Louie,' she adds, as she moves away. 'See you later, Alexander.'

I'm hopping mad, but I can't say anything to Louie. It seems so childish to mind that Louie has met Faye and offered to show her the kittens. Also, I couldn't begin to explain why I am so put out about it: I don't think I understand it myself.

6

The row is blazing as I walk down the stairs, the anger in the air as potent as the smell of smoke. Seth's voice, never quiet at the best of times, is rattling like a machine gun, and replying is Faye's voice, shrill and tearful. For a while I sit on the stairs and listen; because it's great to hear someone else, apart from me, getting it in the neck from a parent.

'Your mother is really upset,' Seth is saying. 'She's accusing me of encouraging you to drop out of school and come over here. You have some explaining to do, young lady.'

'I'm not going back—ever! I don't want to live with Mom and Don any more.'

'It's all arranged, through the court. You can't just cut your mother out. She wants you with her.'

'Mom is a control freak. She just likes the idea of us jumping like little puppets when she pulls the strings. Why can't I do what I want?'

'Because you haven't finished school yet. Why didn't you let her know you were cutting classes and coming here early? You can't just do that, Faye. Now she wants me to stop your allowance. I've had enough hassle with your mother and her lawyers. I don't want any more!'

'I am not going to be shuffled across the Atlantic like some parcel just because you two got divorced. I'm sick of it. For seven years I've gone backwards and forwards like a ping-pong ball. You don't care what it does to my life— or my head.'

'Faye, honey! I don't understand you! You've got it made; you're beautiful, you get good grades at school, you have a nice home . . . a boyfriend. So you spend some time in the States and visit Europe in your holidays. Most kids would see that as an advantage, not something to mope over.'

'I want to be settled and I don't want to live with Mom any more. Don't I get to have a say in what happens to me?'

Faye is really crying hard now and I can hear her sobs: awful animal sounds that make my bare arms goosefleshy. And suddenly I'm sick of sitting on the stairs: I'm cold and I want my breakfast. So I clump down the remaining steps, making enough noise to waken the dead, but they are so busy arguing they don't hear me until I open the kitchen door with a bang.

Seth frowns at me with ill-concealed irritation. Faye doesn't move. When I first look at her I get a really nasty shock because she looks broken; curled up in the old armchair next to the stove with her arms and legs hanging out at awkward angles, as if being uncomfortable doesn't matter to her. She raises her head from the shelter of her arms and seems to register my presence. Then she lowers her face again and hides herself behind her hair. Her face is another shock: red and blotchy with swollen eyes. You would never think that she was pretty if you saw her now! I roll this unkind thought around my head, hoping it will make me feel good: but it doesn't—it makes me feel lousy—and I am suddenly really mad at Seth for making her cry so much.

'Has the world ended or something?' I ask idly, filling the kettle at the sink and switching it on.

'We're having a little crisis,' Seth says, narrowing his eyes at me.

'Oh! What a shame,' I say, filling the toaster with bread. 'Well, as long as you're not launching Cruise missiles on Yorkshire, we should be OK.'

'I'll see you two later,' Seth says wearily. 'Have a nice day,' he adds, as he goes out through the back door.

'World War Three narrowly averted in Yorkshire today!' I mimic, as if I'm reading the news on TV. 'But Yankee man still says: "Have a nice day!" I'd hate to be around when you're having a bad one.' I laugh without humour at my own joke, but Faye doesn't reply.

Even though I make coffee and pour her a cup she still doesn't move. Eventually I finish my breakfast and leave the kitchen. And she is still sitting there, like a doll which has been flung onto the chair and abandoned. There is no reason why she should talk to me about her problems. I haven't given her any reason to think that we might be friends.

The weather is gloomy, in keeping with my mood. There is a low grey sky and a cool wind. The lake is the colour of slate and has little white horses dancing across it. I wonder irritably if they ever have weather two days alike here in Yorkshire, as I go looking for Louie.

There is no sign of her in the field with Fred. I'm too nervous of him to cross the field alone and look around the huts. But I hang about for a bit with my hands thrust deep into the pockets of my jacket, because it really is quite chilly. There are no signs of life, apart from grubby looking towels flapping on the washing line of the cottage and the solitary sound of a rooster crowing.

Eventually I tire of waiting and make for the bus stop. After what seems like hours, a bus finally comes along and I go into Barrowgate. Really, I would rather have gone into Yarham, because that's where Louie is at school and I might have bumped into her, but the bus driver tells me that only the school buses go to Yarham—so it's Barrowgate or nothing.

After looking around the shops I get some fish and chips and sit on the steps and eat them. But it isn't any fun on my own. I think about going back to London and realize I have made a big mistake in bringing all my gear north. It will take an estate car to get it back. To make it worse I remember that Danny's spare room is the size of a cupboard and full of junk—wine-making equipment and collections of fossils—really important stuff. So I don't know where I will put my books and things when I get there. The attic back at the cottage suddenly seems palatial in comparison.

Eventually I realize that there is no point in hanging around Barrowgate like a moron. What I really need to do is to go home and get on with some work. I curse Faye—because I got out of the house largely to get away from her. I don't know why I find her so distracting. When she's in the house, even when we're not in the same room, I find I can't stop thinking about her, and listening for her.

When I get back to the village, having waited another hour for a bus, I find I'm still reluctant to go home. My feet take over and lead me again to Fred's field. Louie is there. She is pale and has dark circles under her eyes.

'You look rough. What've you been up to?' As soon as I've said it, I realize it's the kind of remark I might make to Danny or Jean-Paul, but isn't the greatest chat up line to use with a girl.

Louie groans and pulls a face: 'I'm knackered. I didn't get too much sleep last night. Then my mam got me up at dawn and ordered me off to school. I'm just about to feed the birds. Want to come?'

Fred really biffs me with his big head, nearly knocking me off my feet, as he tries to get the carrots out of my pocket. I'm quite chuffed because I'm not really scared any more, just a bit nervous, and I even manage to pat his neck.

First we feed the puppies. I hold my favourite one again, resting my cheek against the warm biscuit-smelling fur, as the little dog chews on my fingers with tiny, white-splinter teeth.

Then Louie takes me to see the birds. 'This one is a

cock pheasant . . . ' she explains. 'And this is a hen. I'm hoping she'll be able to go back into the wild, her wing is mending well. But old Sparky will have to stay here with me. He's got a gammy leg and a broken wing. He wouldn't last five minutes—the fox would have him. I try not to handle the ones that are likely to go back, but he's a real pet now. Here, give him some corn.'

When I reach inside the run the bird swivels his head and tries to peck me and I withdraw my hand quickly. Louie shakes her head with disbelief at my cowardice. Conscious of her amused eyes on me, I try again, and don't flinch when the bird pecks the corn from my palm, even though the sensation is far from pleasant.

'I can't believe they live wild in the woods here,' I say wonderingly. 'He's so exotic, the amazing colours on him and the little ears at the side of his head.'

'They're bred by the gamekeepers and set free so they can be shot, but some live wild and breed. I really hate shooting and hunting—and the prats who do it,' Louie adds with a yawn.

'Why were you up so late?' I ask curiously. 'Not more puppies?'

'No!' Louie says curtly. 'Ask no questions you'll get told no lies . . . ' she adds dismissively, turning her back on me.

'Well, I'll be off,' I say miserably. I've been waiting all day to have someone to talk to, but Louie seems in a bad mood. She follows me out of the hut.

'I'm all in,' she says gruffly.

'That's all right,' I say, even though it isn't. I want someone to talk and laugh with. But today Louie seems locked in some private world that I know nothing about.

'Thanks for lunch yesterday. I was that pogged I couldn't eat another thing all day.' Then she adds: 'Tell you what, Alex, if you want to come out one night, I'll show you something special.'

'OK,' I say nonchalantly. 'If you like.' But I cannot stop a little spiral of pleasure uncurling inside me. This is, after all, the first time any girl has ever asked me out.

'Ever seen a badger?' she asks.

'Only a stuffed one in a museum.'

Louie crinkles up her nose: 'Yuk! I hate museums and things in glass cases. It's horrible keeping dead things like that. They all want burying.'

'I don't suppose you like zoos either, do you?'

'No. I don't like animals kept in cages,' she says. 'And it's wrong to keep polar bears and things in warm climates, it's cruel.'

'Yes, I suppose so.' I can think of lots of arguments for the keeping of animals in captivity but I don't feel like spoiling this conversation.

Moving closer to me she says in a slow, soft voice: 'I've found a badger sett and they've got young 'uns. If you promise not to tell anyone where they are I'll take you to see them.'

'Yes, that would be great.' I can see by the look on her face that this is a big deal for her and I am flattered that she has asked me.

'Tomorrow night? In the churchyard at eleven. Will you be able to get out?'

'Yes, of course,' I say quickly. 'I'm going away to university soon. My mother doesn't keep me on a lead.'

She grins and turns away. 'See you, then,' she says, and is gone.

The cottage is cold and dark. First of all I light the stove and make some coffee, then I phone Danny. I can't get a signal on my mobile so I have to ring him on the old phone in the hall. We have a good crack about school and what everyone is doing. It's great to hear all the news, but to be honest it makes me kind of lonely to hear about it all.

'Any nice girls up there?' Danny asks with a laugh.

'I'm fighting them off, mate,' I joke, then I add, more seriously. 'There's a great kid who lives down the road. She's called Louie and she's an original. An eco-warrior. Tomorrow night we're going out to see badgers. Yes, of course wild ones, you pillock. This is the country with a capital C. It's like the land that time forgot. Yeah, come and visit if you want. I've got a great attic. Plenty of room.'

The thought of Danny coming up here is great. I wouldn't mind sharing Louie with him. I think they'd hit it off. Danny always eats up any food put in front of him and is dead keen on animals. He and Louie would have a lot in common.

While I'm still on the phone to Danny I hear someone come into the kitchen. We leave the back door unlocked, it's not like London at all. I try Jean-Paul's number but no one is at home. I'm sorry—because J-P wants to be a psychiatrist and he is great to talk to about Hardy and serious stuff. I wouldn't mind Faye overhearing me talking heavy duty intellectualism with him.

When I get back into the kitchen Little Miss Efficiency is busy unpacking shopping. 'Was there anything left at Sainsburys?' I ask mockingly. 'Looks like you did a trolley dash.'

'Hi, Alexander,' she says a little warily. 'I got you some perishables while I was out.' Reaching into one of the bags she places two large wholemeal loaves and a bag of carrots on the table. 'And I got you some apples as well. Although I wasn't sure which kind you like.'

'Any kind at all,' I say brusquely. I know I must say thank you to her but the words seem to have got stuck somewhere in my chest and will not come out. 'How much do I owe you?' I ask stiffly.

'It was only a couple of pounds and it really doesn't matter. Seth gave me plenty of housekeeping money. And I just thought if you had your own supply it might help things along with Diane . . . ' She gives me this hopeful, pleading kind of look.

'Because we mustn't upset Mumsie, must we?' I retort angrily. 'It will take more than extra bread and veg to make *her* happy.'

'Alexander, please,' Faye says. Her tone is firm, as if I am still at Junior School and need straightening out. It makes me want to puke especially when she continues: 'I don't think you've realized how hard Diane is working. She is starting a new job and a new relationship. And this house is very difficult to run. I just want things to go smoothly for her, and for all of us to have a good summer.'

I really resent being told how to treat my own mother and wonder, in a moment of fury, if Seth has asked her to speak to me.

'I suppose you think if you creep around them enough they won't send you home?' I sneer. 'Well, I tell you something, Miss Goody Two Shoes, I wish they would send me home. I can't wait to get away from this dump! I'm off to London as soon as I can get my stuff shifted.'

She looks at me very calmly, which makes me even more angry. My face is burning with temper, but she is completely composed and in charge, and it makes me want to throw something at her.

'You must do what you want, Alexander. But while you are here you might try to be polite to everyone. You may have reasons for being angry with your mother but I don't see what Seth and I have done to deserve . . . '

'Don't preach to me . . . ' I snarl at her. I would like to tell her about my mother renting out our home without even asking me—and about how Mandy and Dad make me feel like an interloper when I'm with them—but this great big wave of misery suddenly engulfs me so I feel like crying. I storm out of the kitchen and stamp up the stairs.

Throwing myself down on the bed I reach for my book.

Then I finish reading Hardy's *Jude the Obscure*—every miserable word of it. The bit where all those poor little children are murdered is so awful I don't mind that my eyes prickle and my throat aches. It's like having a long hot bath in someone else's misery and I get so involved I don't realize that the day is darkening early and my room is too gloomy for reading in comfort. It is only when I finally surface from *Jude* that I also become aware of a delicious smell emanating from the kitchen: fried onions and freshly baked bread. My stomach rumbles noisily in the silence of the room. And, even though I had intended to stay in my room all evening, the aroma of the food lures me downstairs.

Seth and my mother have arrived home. They are drinking wine and laughing. Faye, wearing a crisp blue and white apron, is dishing up food.

'Good, you've come down for supper,' she says with a smile. She acts as if nothing has happened between us, laughing, even calling me 'Alexander, honey'. She fusses over me too, giving me more sauce on my spaghetti and refilling my glass with Aqua Libra, like she's Wendy and I'm her Peter Pan.

'Tomorrow night we've all been invited to a party,' Seth says, grinning at me. 'Up at The Grange—the big house on the top of the hill. The kids there are going to have a marquee in the garden—should be good!'

'I'm busy . . . ' I mumble, through a mouthful of pasta.

'Don't be so ridiculous. You can't possibly be busy,' my mother snaps.

'Alexander has a cute friend called Louie,' Faye says diplomatically. 'Maybe she could come to the party too.'

Looking up from my food I stare hard at her, hoping that hatred is radiating from my eyes: 'Are you cracked or something?' I ask rudely.

'Alex!' my mother hisses. Then her eyes narrow.

'Why wouldn't Louie want to come . . . I hope you're not . . .'

'Finding someone unsuitable to be friends with,' I end the sentence for her, my voice a shrill mimic of hers. 'Yes, mother dear, Louie is totally wild and leading me into all kinds of bad ways.'

'As a favour, could you come to the party for a little while, to keep me company, before you go out with Louie?' Faye asks me. She gives me this lovely smile, full of confidence and kindness. Oh-my-god . . . what would Danny or Jean-Paul say if she asked them to go to a party with her?

There is a long silence. I don't answer.

She shrugs her shoulders apologetically: 'I'm still jet lagged. I don't really want to party. We could just stay for an hour, to be polite. Come to the party with me, please, Alexander?'

Her voice, and the logic of this plan, sets my teeth on edge. Little Miss Organized! And some part of me, my strong male side, wants very much to hurt her. I am poised to make a really hateful remark because she has laid herself open to me, like an animal who lies down and exposes its soft underbelly, and it's going to be so very good to kick her and watch her squirm. And somehow I know that when I have rejected this advance of friendship she will never try again.

There are so many cruel remarks jostling in my mind that I pause, savouring the moment.

'Don't bother to be nice to him,' my mother butts in. I can see from the slight looseness of her mouth that she has drunk too much wine.

'And why not?' I snap.

'Because it's a waste of time,' she retorts.

'Diane, please . . . This is between Alexander and me.' Faye is gracious but firm. 'It's nothing to do with you or Seth. Please, just leave us alone.'

Faye starts to clear the table, but all the time she is watching me, waiting for me to speak.

Seth has lost interest in us; he gets hold of my mother's arm, pulls her into an embrace and kisses her mouth. I turn away with distaste. No one is going to be listening to me: my moment has passed. So I say, in a suitably dull, noncommittal sort of voice, 'OK. I'll come to the party for an hour. But I'm actually here to work, not to have fun.'

'I shouldn't worry, Alexander, I don't think there's any danger of you having *too* much fun partying with me,' Faye says drily, and I find I'm smiling in spite of myself.

The next day it's warm and sunny. Seth isn't filming and so the three of them go off to visit Whitby. I would have rather liked to have gone too, because it's the place where Bram Stoker got the idea for *Dracula,* but I can't face a day in the company of all of them. Especially as Faye has taken a camera and a camcorder. Trailing around with them would just be so embarrassing. So I stay at the cottage on my own.

In the morning I go down and feed the goats: I can't believe how much bread they can put away. Then I make myself comfortable in the garden and write an essay on the Wars of the Roses for history and a question on the spirit of redemption in Thomas Hardy's novels for English. I actually think the poor old sod needed Prozac and wonder, rather gloomily, if manic depression is a necessary prerequisite for creative genius. If so, I think I'll give up any idea of writing a novel: I'd rather be happy.

In the evening I get myself dressed for going to see badgers and not for a party. My mother looks at my jeans, T-shirt, and Doc Martens with a little moue of horror.

'Can't you please put on something clean, Alex? We *are* going out.'

'Really, Diane, he looks fine,' Faye intercedes quickly. Of course, Little Miss Barbie is looking fabulous, dolled up in a silk dress that clings around her arms and legs like a multicoloured cloud. 'Boys don't dress up for social occasions. It's not cool,' she adds with a little laugh.

We walk up to The Grange, my mother teetering on high heels and grabbing hold of Seth's arm. Even before we reach the house I'm wishing I hadn't agreed to come. The Grange is a big, square, grey, stone house built by some eccentric Victorian as a mini castle with fake turrets and a flagpole, and it looks like a setting for an Agatha Christie murder mystery.

The big iron-studded front door leads into a wood-panelled hallway which has several stags' heads and stuffed pike in glass cases on the walls. It's all utterly grotesque and would make Louie sick. The doors are open into the reception rooms which are full to bursting with middle-aged people holding huge glasses of wine and shouting at each other. The music is some old crooner from the 1950s singing a love song to his girl. I sigh loudly, thinking that lying in my attic reading another Hardy novel would be a riot compared to this.

An old woman comes rushing up to us, smiling and flashing huge yellow teeth: 'Seth, how wonderful that you could come . . . And this must be Diane, and Faye, your daughter. We are delighted to meet you all.' Then she turns to me, her hand outstretched: 'And this *must* be the boyfriend from America . . . How lovely!'

Faye and I both open our mouths to speak, but I get in first. My voice is a great bellow as I reach out for the old woman's wrinkled, bejewelled paw and begin to pump it up and down:

'Howdy, Mam, I'm Randy, from Houston, Texas. Great to be in your little old country.'

Never for a moment do I expect her to be taken in by my impression. I mean it would be obvious to a child of five that I am doing a bad impression of an American, hooting out Houston and leering at her like some old phoney.

But she trills: 'Randy . . . how lovely. Do come and

meet everyone.' Taking my arm, she calls into the kitchen: 'Amber, Sarah . . . do come and meet Randy. He's from Texas.'

As I am whirled away, I register my mother's furious face, Seth's blank expression, and Faye's bewildered look. I realize that we have only just arrived and I have already managed to spoil the evening for them.

7

The two girls I have been handed over to fasten themselves to me like prison warders, I don't need a straitjacket, they are standing so close I can hardly breathe. They keep on asking me questions which I can't answer. I'm not really very good at accents and so I have to reply by nodding or shaking my head and saying things like: 'Sure thing, buddy . . . ' I also smile a lot.

They lead me through the kitchen and out to the back garden of the house where there is a huge marquee. One section has a bar and a table covered with food and the other section is a disco. The disco area is rather dark and the music is very loud. Somehow I think I'd be better off in there but my two captors are plying me with food and shrieking to people as they pass by:

'This is Randy from Texas, say hello to him.' There are a few sniggers from people because of the name, but most are really friendly and stop and speak to me.

'We must get Randy a drink . . . ' They haul me off to the bar. I refuse the fruit cup which has been made up in a huge silver bowl and has leaves and chunks of fruit floating around in it.

'You got a 'gator in there?' I ask suspiciously.

The girls find this hilarious and scream with laughter. One of them shouts across the room: 'Guess what, Jane? Randy's just asked if there's an alligator in the punch bowl!'

At that moment Faye walks up and takes hold of my arm.

'Come and dance, please,' she says, and the girls slink away like two hyenas disturbed at the kill by a lioness. I grin and follow her into the disco.

The DJ is playing some terrible old Beatles record and all the couples are smooching. Faye puts her arms up against my chest and asks in a whisper: 'Are you going to keep this stupid pretence up all night?'

'Sure thing, honey!' I say loudly into her ear.

'Why?'

'Because it amuses me,' I say in my own voice.

'And that is enough of a reason, is it?' she asks quietly.

'Oh come on, Faye. It's only a bit of a joke,' I reply irritably.

'I think it's very impolite. How are these people going to feel when they find out?'

I put my arms around her as I say: 'I'm going to be legging it back to London as soon as I can. I'm only going to have a couple of beers and then I'm leaving. Just cool it. OK?'

She is stiff, like a cardboard cut-out in my arms. I am suddenly aware that I am hugging her very close and try to loosen my grip. I'm not very good at dancing and we are struggling to move in time to the music, but my arms seem to have a life of their own and will not release her.

Then the realization that I *want* to hold her close hits me like a bad tackle on a football pitch. For a moment I am dazed. All the previous longings in my life pale and disappear in comparison with this surge of wanting. I have her locked in an embrace like a demented grizzly. When the music finally stops it is only by some supreme effort of will power that I drop my arms and move away from her.

To cover my confusion I shout loudly in my best 'Randy' voice: 'Let me get you a drink, sweetheart,' as I march her off the dance floor.

When we get to the bar I hiss in her ear, 'Give the fruit cup a miss.' Then I ask the bartender for two cold beers.

'I don't like beer,' she says, helping herself to the punch. I shrug and, grabbing the two bottles, wander off. I feel a bit of a fool walking around on my own, so I dive into the disco where it is dark and drink one of the bottles. The liquor is cool in my throat, splendidly bitter.

Faye comes into the disco with a tall boy. He has long rather floppy hair and a well-chiselled face. He and Faye are deep in conversation and she is swigging fruit cup like it's Ribena. And all the time he is talking to her, his face is very close to hers. When she finishes her drink they start jigging around on the dance floor. She dances beautifully, but then it's easy for girls. She wiggles and shimmies and the flowing silk of her skirt whirls in time with the music. It's magic to watch and I know I am not the only person entranced by her. She looks gorgeous—whereas her partner looks like a stick insect who's just got a whiff of insecticide—one more spasm and he'll be a goner . . .

'I see Leo has pulled someone new . . . ' I hear a female voice muttering from behind me and I nearly choke on a swig of beer. Leo—what a name! What a prat! I start on my second bottle of beer and watch Faye and Leo having another drink. He has his arm around her shoulders now and is nuzzling her ear as if he hasn't had a square meal in months and is about to devour her. The beer is fizzing inside my mouth and I have a sudden desire to spit.

Leaving the marquee, I walk around under the trees for a while until I find a garden bench to lie down on. Above me the night sky is like an illustration from a child's story book: a gigantic arc of pure black velvet adorned with a white shiny moon. I lie there for ages looking at the stars twinkling and winking at me. The beer has filled my stomach and made me feel contented, like a baby ready for sleep.

When I go back to the disco Faye and Leo are dancing again. He keeps on grabbing at her and whirling her around. I can see she doesn't like it. She looks kind of tired and hot, but he keeps on doing it, and I can't understand why he can't see that she isn't happy. I feel like walking up to him and giving him a shove. Just as this urge is becoming irresistible, a little red-haired girl with a big smile comes bouncing up to me.

'Hello! You're Randy, aren't you? Would you like to dance?' she asks.

Considering how small she is she has a really deep, very posh voice. Now I am back inside, in the heat and the noise, I feel a bit tired and depressed so I just smile in reply and follow her onto the dance floor. There isn't much room so I just bob about a bit. The red-haired girl is prancing around in front of me. And when the music slows down she hurtles into my arms and wraps herself around me, as if she is a boa-constrictor on heat. I am astonished and it takes a few moments for me to persuade myself that I am enjoying the experience.

'Looks like you lost your girlfriend to Leo,' she sniggers into my ear. I glance around at Faye and Leo, who are now dancing very close together, and shrug. 'Isn't it a big thing between you two?' the ginger kid questions. I shrug again. 'That's good!' she adds. Her arms wrap around my neck like a hangman's rope and she pulls my head down to her level. Then I can feel her lips moving against mine.

Now I have nothing against women's liberation and all that stuff. It's fine by me if women want to be airline pilots or anything they want. They can box or go down coal mines for all I care. But I've always thought that when I got around to a bit of proper passion, I would be the one calling the shots. I feel an absolute fool standing in this crowd of people with this little red-haired dwarfy thing trying to put her tongue in my mouth. I mean, now I know how girls must feel when they get groped by blokes they don't like. I don't even know this girl's name, for crying out loud! So what makes her think I want to snog her?

Just as I am trying to entangle her arms from around my neck, I hear a kind of squeal from behind me. I know in an instant that it's Faye and I grab hold of the red-haired girl's arms and throw her off me. When I turn around I see Faye looking dazed and Leo staring at her.

'Where I come from boys do *not* do that to girls when they are dancing!' Faye says loudly. Then she staggers a bit and puts her hands up over her face.

'She's drunk . . . ' the red-haired girl laughs. 'Leo's hip flask at work again.'

Elbowing my way through the crowd I grab hold of Faye's arm. Then, dragging her behind me, I shoulder my way through all the people who are staring at us and get her out into the garden.

The fresh air hits her like a slap in the face and she staggers against me like a toddler knocked off balance. I straighten her up.

'Alexander . . . I feel terrible . . . I feel so dizzy and sick . . . ' she says in this really puzzled voice.

'You're drunk,' I retort. 'Come on.' I take hold of her arm again, only more gently this time. 'I'll take you home.'

'But I don't drink . . . ' she mutters. 'I only had fruit cup . . . '

'And the rest,' I say unsympathetically. 'Come on— we're leaving.'

I don't want to take her through the house, so I make a detour through the garden.

'Are we going the right way? It's so dark . . . ' she complains, as she weaves and stumbles next to me. The lawn is damp and slippery with dew and the slope is steep. We lose our footing at the same moment and grab at each other, before going over like ice-skaters. I land on my knees and get up pretty quickly but Faye is spread-eagled like a cartoon character.

'Come on, Faye. Get up,' I say, pulling at her hand. At first I think she is giggling, but then I realize she is crying.

I haul her to her feet and wrap my arm tightly around her waist. Then we stumble down the hill together like children in a three-legged race.

By the time we reach the cottage we are like conjoined twins, a warm damp area of comfort binds us together. It seems that we have always been linked like this and when I loosen my grip on her I feel bereft and naked.

Sitting her down next to the Rayburn I get some kitchen roll and try to wipe her tear-stained face. All the time she keeps on saying she is sorry and it makes me feel awful. I keep thinking about what a good time we could have had, if only that old woman hadn't assumed I was Erik.

'Don't cry. It doesn't matter, honestly. Please don't keep saying you're sorry, or I'll go back and ram Leo's hip flask down his throat.'

'What?' she asks, bemused.

'He must have been putting something in your drink to get you as plastered as this, mustn't he?'

Her head bows and she weeps afresh. I don't know what to say to make it better, but I notice that her elbow is bleeding and there is blood on my T-shirt and down the front of her dress. So I get a bowl of hot water and bathe her arm—just like I remember my mother doing for me when I was small—dabbing the cut with Dettol and patting it dry.

When I have finished, I lean back on my heels and smile at her, rather pleased with myself. 'Would you like a hot drink?' I ask solicitously.

'A coffee, please. You've been so kind. Thank you.'

Her hands shake a bit as she takes the coffee but she is sobering up quite well, which is good because I would hate to have the responsibility of putting someone who is drunk to bed. I'd be scared they'd choke on their own vomit or something like that. It happened to a friend's older brother when we were in the first year at secondary school. This guy, he was called Spencer

Johns, went out for a curry and few pints. He must have had too much beer because his mum found him dead in bed in the morning. It frightened the life out of me. I think that's probably why I've never had more than three pints.

Anyway Faye is coming round quite well; she sits and looks down into the mug of coffee and there is a long silence between us. But it isn't irksome, one of those pauses when you rack your brain for something to say. It's the silence you get between friends, or people who are at ease with each other.

Eventually I say: 'So you didn't fancy old Leo then?' I don't really know how I have the cheek to ask her a question like that—it's so completely personal—but it's very important for me to know if she really liked Leo or not. I'm not quite sure why I have to know, but I do. 'I didn't spoil things for you, did I?' I ask.

She looks up from her coffee and our eyes meet. 'No, Alexander, you didn't spoil things for me. Quite the opposite. You saved my life.' She says this really seriously, as if she really means it, and I laugh to hide my embarrassment.

'I suppose it could get difficult, when Erik the American heart-throb arrives. I can see the headlines already. *Love triangle in Yorkshire dales.* We don't want you getting into the *News of the World*.'

She looks puzzled and I explain about the Sunday papers in England. I'm talking now to fill the silence because I know the next thing she will tell me is when Erik is arriving and I don't want to hear it.

Eventually, when there is a pause in my account of tabloid journalism, she says quickly, 'Erik won't be coming here, not now, not ever. It really is over between us.'

'I see,' I say flatly. The words 'I'm sorry' get lost in my brain and do not surface. When I look closely I see that her eyes are brimming with tears and I move swiftly, like an anxious parent, grabbing more kitchen roll and sitting

80

down at her feet. Mopping her face I say soothingly, 'Don't get upset. It's not the end of the world.'

'Oh, Alexander . . . ' she says with a sob. 'I've made such a mess of my life. And tonight, when I realized how smashed I was, I felt as if I had become the very person I have always hated.'

'And who's that?'

'My mom,' she whispers.

'Doesn't that happen to everyone?' I ask. 'As Oscar Wilde said: "All women become like their mothers. That is their tragedy. No man does. That is his." I find that a comforting thought sometimes. Especially when I look at my mother!'

'You're very clever,' she says, blowing her nose on the kitchen roll and giving me a ghost of a smile. 'But Diane isn't that bad, you know.'

'Are things really grim at home? Is that why you don't want to live with your mother any more?' I ask, and Faye nods.

'I really wanted to go with Pop when he left. I think my mother would have let me go—if she had thought I wanted to stay with her. But as soon as she knew Pop and I wanted to be together she dug her heels in and demanded I stay with her. There was a very acrimonious court case. They argue constantly over access to me. You would think I was really precious to them.'

'Well, aren't you?' I ask puzzled. As I see it Faye is everything, and I mean everything, I am not. I could imagine parents fighting to the death over her.

Shaking her head she says sadly, 'They give me everything . . . all the things which money can buy. But none of the things which come free in a happy home.'

There is a pause and then she continues: 'There is this girl, called Monica, who has come up through school with me and if school is a wolf pack then she is Omega wolf.' Looking across at me she explains, 'The head of the pack is the Alpha. The bravest, brightest, and best.'

I don't say: 'That would be you,' but I think it and I get the feeling that Faye knows that thought is in my head. It's a weird feeling, this idea she can read my mind. 'Go on . . . ' I mutter.

'At the bottom of the pack is the Omega, the one who is always picked on. Well, at school it was poor old Monica. The hardest kids were awful to her and the rest of us just ignored her. She was the one who always got dud grades, had acne and the biggest retainer in the world. Everyone else dated, and went on parties and picnics, but not Monica. She just got greyer and more transparent over the years, so that eventually even the bullying stopped. It was just as if she didn't exist for the rest of us. Then one day, in the spring, I found her library book. It was the last day of school and I knew she would be in trouble if she didn't return it. So I called at her house. I'd just passed my test and Pop had bought me a red roadster. I suppose I wanted to show it off as much as anything.' Faye chews her lip as if this is some awful confession.

'Well,' I say gently. 'I expect most people would feel like that with their first car. At least you didn't just throw her book in the rubbish bin.'

'Monica and her family were packing up their car to go on vacation. I mean I'd always known that Monica didn't come from a rich family or anything. But they were loading up this real old station wagon with these really terrible suitcases. There were these two little kids, a dog, boxes of groceries—just so much stuff! And Monica's mom stopped everything when I arrived and insisted I go inside for coffee and cookies. And the little kids and Monica sat and watched me like I was something from Mars. Monica's mom kept saying how nice it was to meet one of Monica's friends at last. Like she had no idea that Monica didn't have a friend, had never had a friend, in all the years we had been at school together.'

Faye drains her coffee and I take the mug from her hands and put it down on the floor next to the stove. 'Then they started telling me about their holiday and the little kids talked about Monica. How she took them canoeing and lit camp fires with them. And it hit me that to those two kids Monica was a star. And then they all tumbled out of their junky house and waved me goodbye. And when I drove away I had tears in my heart because I wanted to be Monica. Me, Faye McElroy, wanted to swap places with Monica . . . And I don't really understand why . . . '

'Because she isn't an *einzelkind* . . . ' I say gently.

'What's that?' Faye wrinkles her nose at me.

'Only child. Parents divorce. Suddenly—no family. No one at all.'

'You're so wise, Alexander. How come you worked it all out and it never occurred to me that I was lacking something? I suppose I was too busy believing my own publicity and having a good time.' She gives me a little sideways look and continues in a rush. 'Only it wasn't a good time. It was all a lie.'

'All of it?' I ask gently.

'Especially Erik.' It's as if she knew what I wanted to ask. 'I got involved with him so darned quickly. Like I thought that he was what I had been looking for all my life.'

She doesn't cry, and she doesn't look at me, she stares down at the rug and carries on talking, her voice quick and low.

'He said he loved me and I really, really believed it. I suppose I thought that finally someone loved me for myself. And so I gave him everything. Every little part of my body and soul. All those special secrets that are so precious. I just handed myself over.'

'Did he let you down?'

'Yes . . . ' she nods. 'He found someone else. And the most terrible thing was I realized that I hadn't been in love with him at all. I think I was just in love with the idea of love. I grew not just to despise him but to actually dislike him. He's shallow and vain and deeply stupid. Not at all the kind of guy I had thought I would give my virginity to.'

Looking away abruptly I am ashamed of the heat rising to my face. I had realized what we were talking about, but I hadn't expected her to be quite so open with me about it.

'Never mind. Plenty more fish in the sea . . . ' I mutter.

She reaches out and touches my arm and I look up and meet her eyes.

'Please don't say that, Alexander. That was what my mother said to me. And I don't want to be like her, stumbling through life from one dead-end relationship to another.'

'You could join a nunnery,' I say jokingly, and then, because I don't want to hurt her feelings, I reach out and put my arms around her and hold her close against my chest. And this time my arms are gentle and she is soft and fragile, like something which needs looking after. 'I'm glad you're not Monica, anyway. I like you just the way you are,' I mutter, my voice thick with embarrassment and emotion.

We stay like that for some time, not moving, just resting in each other's arms until our breathing slows and becomes like one.

'Alexander . . . ' she says finally, her voice a slow whisper, as if she is sleepy. 'If Seth and Diane decide to marry we'll be . . . kind of like brother and sister.'

'Yes . . . ' I say, trying not to sound uncertain. Then with new authority I add: 'Come on, you're nearly asleep. Time for bed.'

'Alexander,' she says, concerned. 'What's the time? Have you missed your date with Louie?'

Looking up at the clock, I see that it is eleven thirty and I doubt very much if Louie will have waited.

'Oh hell,' I mutter. Then I add quickly: 'I'll explain. I'm sure Louie will understand.' I don't add that Louie knows all about the importance of looking after things which are precious.

84

'It wasn't really a date,' I reassure her. 'Louie was going to take me to see a badger sett. If you like, when we go, you could come with us.' I hold this offer out like a white flag of truce: the final seal of our friendship.

'Do you mean it? I'd love that—truly I would,' she says, in her lovely sincere American way.

'Good. I'll try to catch up with Louie tomorrow.'

We walk up the stairs, not holding hands, but not apart either: our arms and shoulders touching as we go. At the top I mumble a farewell and climb up to my attic. I don't know if my heart is breaking, or melting, or singing with joy. I don't know if I'm happy or sad. If I'm in love or just bemused. All I do know is that I am brimming with emotion and feelings, so that my skin feels tingly and my eyes bright and sharp with unshed tears.

Opening the skylight window I stick my head through and gulp down the clean night air. Then, leaving the window open, I curl under the duvet and look up at the night sky. These are the same stars which winked and twinkled down at me when I lay on the bench in the garden of The Grange. Yet I'm different. I'm changed. In some wonderful, magical way I've finally grown up.

8

In the morning, when I wake up, I hear all the birds singing—it's amazingly loud and tuneful—like a bird orchestra. For a while I lie in bed just thinking about Leo, the red-haired girl, and Erik. I wish the whole world would disappear and leave me and Faye alone. If it were possible I would transport us to a tropical island where we would be marooned.

Leaning from the window I look out at the dew-drenched valley. The lake is a thread of silver ribbon in a web of mist. I know what this morning haze means—it will be hot later—it gives me a kick to know I can predict the weather.

From below me I can hear the urgent hum of voices, an ugly sound like a mosquito caught under a sheet.

Retrieving last night's jeans and T-shirt from the floor I pull them on. Then I creep down the stairs, wary and alert. The first thing I see when I walk into the kitchen is Faye's silk dress from the night before spread out on the back of one of the chairs. It's an awful shock to see it there: it looks terrible, there's a rip along the hem, it's covered in grass stains and there's blood down the front.

As I walk into the room Seth turns and stares at me. He is completely stressed out: like a violin string that has been over-tightened. He looks like a man ready for a fight and I edge into the room carefully and make my way over to the sink.

'Morning . . .' I murmur, reaching for the kettle.

Seth moves next to me with the speed and silence of a

mountain cat. He doesn't touch me, but his closeness is so intimidating my hands drop to my sides as I turn and confront him.

'What's up?' I ask, wishing my voice didn't sound so nervous.

'What did you do to my little girl last night?' he hisses at me.

'Seth, please . . . let me handle this,' my mother says quickly. She has risen to her feet. I briefly register she is still in her dressing-gown and her face is pale and creased as if she has missed her beauty sleep.

'I want to know!' Seth breathes heavily into my face. He completely ignores my mother. Instead he fixes me with this terrible stare: his dark eyes are glinting with purple lights this morning. Suddenly he gives me a shoulder barge and I jump away from him as if he has thrown a thousand volts through my body.

'What on earth is the matter with you?' I snap. I want to shout at him to leave me alone and keep his distance. I hate his physicality and masculinity. I hate the idea that he thinks he can talk to me like this. And it freaks me that he and my mother are ganging up on me.

'Tell me what happened last night,' he says through clenched teeth.

Moving away from him I say coolly: 'I don't know what you're talking about,' because I don't see why I have to answer to him.

'You've had some goddam chip on your shoulder about my little girl from the second she arrived. You've never said one polite word to her. You've put her down, you've insulted her. You goddam son-of-a—'

'Seth, please, let me . . . ' my mother tries to butt in.

'You've taken every opportunity to abuse my baby . . . ' Seth rages at me. 'And then you take her off. You drag her out of the party. Don't think we haven't been told about it. And then she comes home with her clothes all ripped. What the hell did you do to her? You creepy little pervert!

Does it give you a thrill to hurt girls? You want locking up!'

He comes towards me, his arms swinging, his face contorted with fury: 'If you've touched my baby I'll kill you, you little . . . '

But I don't give him a chance to finish. Picking up a chair I hold it out in front of me as if I'm a lion tamer and he some ravenous beast of prey. I don't fancy getting my teeth knocked out by him.

'Listen to me, you stupid moronic Yank!' I yell at him, my voice suddenly loud and aggressive. 'I wouldn't hurt Faye. But I'll hurt you, you thick-skulled idiot, if you lay a finger on me. You must be mad to jump to conclusions like this. You haven't the brains you were born with.'

'You think you're so damned smart . . . ' he growls at me, edging around the legs of the chair. 'Such a clever guy . . . '

'Well, compared to you I am,' I retort swiftly. 'You're making a complete prawn-ball of yourself!'

'How did her clothes get so dirty? Was it you, messing with her?'

Into my mind comes the image of Faye in my arms, and fury overcomes me like a muscle spasm. I can't control it—it's like being caught by some gigantic breaker when paddling in the sea.

'Shut up!' I yell. 'Or I'll mess with you!' I lunge forward with the chair. 'You over-sexed gorilla! Just because you can't keep your filthy hands off my mother you think . . . '

He doesn't let me finish. He jerks the chair from my hands and makes for my throat. My mother screams and then everything goes black.

In films and action novels people get knocked out then they are fine: they bounce back like tennis balls and carry on shooting, fighting, or jumping off cliffs. In reality being knocked out cold makes you feel as if you are going to die.

I surface from some deep terrible slumber to find myself lying on the cold stone flags of the floor. The room is full of ghastly noise that sends splinters of pain right through my skull. I groan and try to move.

'He's coming round . . . ' I hear my mother sob.

'Don't let him move until the ambulance comes,' Faye wails. It's terrible to hear her crying like this. When I sit up I find my stomach is heaving and my mouth doesn't belong to me any more. I am aware of Faye holding me and of her voice crooning in some loving lament. It is this which gives me the strength to stand up.

'I don't need a bloody ambulance . . . ' I say loudly.

'You've been unconscious . . . ' she sobs, trying to take me in her arms again.

'No I haven't. I was only mucking about. Let me alone.' I shrug her away. Then I get up and stagger to the door. My mother and Seth are watching me in stunned disbelief: their mouths round, black holes in their ashen faces.

Slamming the door behind me I walk as quickly as I can on my unsteady legs down the lane. In the distance I can hear the waa-waa of an emergency ambulance. Let Seth sort that one out!

Near to the lake the damp air swirls around me like a flimsy white shroud, cold as the kiss of a corpse. I go down to the church, hoping the goats will be there, but there is no sign of them. I huddle in the porch for a while, safe in the knowledge that no one will look for me here.

The chill air gets to me, my stomach is turning somersaults and I crave company. So I walk quickly through the churchyard and down to the woods, swinging my arms to get warm, hoping that Louie is at home.

Fred seems to sense that I'm feeling fragile. He comes across to me as I climb over the gate and snorts gently through his nose, fanning my face with warm, grass-sweet breath, but he doesn't knock me, or try to get to my pockets. Instead he walks very carefully next to me as I trudge up the field.

Louie and Blue are in the shed with the puppies. 'What the hell are you doing here? You're only eight hours late,' she asks with a scowl. Then she moves across to me, concern on her face: 'Are you all right, Alex? You look like death warmed up. Did you get plastered last night?'

'I banged my head and I haven't had any breakfast,' I mumble.

'Or any sleep by the look of you. Teach you to have a skinful,' Louie says with a dismissive shrug. Then she looks more closely at me and says: 'Let's have a look at your head.'

She deals with me with all the efficiency that she uses with the animals. With gentle hands she bathes the lump on my head with icy water and she makes little tutting sounds of comfort as she settles me down under the tree on an old blanket with a feed sack for a pillow.

'Lie down there. I'll go and sweet-talk Mam into giving us some rations. She's baking this morning. You picked a good day to be an invalid. Do you want a cup of tea? I was just going to have one.'

I know now why old Fred whinnies with love and gratitude when he sees her.

'You'd make a great nurse,' I mumble.

'I'd rather be a vet,' Louie says.

Blue assumes the rug has been put down for him. He stretches himself next to me and goes to sleep and I curl into the warmth of his body.

Louie disappears off to the cottage and comes back with a tin tray. On it are two thick, chipped mugs full of very sweet tea and some crunchy hot scones spread with marg. Normally I never take sugar in drinks but that tea is like nectar.

I lie down again on the rug. Louie lets the kittens out and grooms each one carefully with an old toothbrush. Then they come over and clamber on me. I feel their little paws and claws and smell the warm milky smell of them. Opening my eyes I see tabby fur and whiskers. Then one of the bolder kittens comes up and licks my face with a tiny sandpapery tongue. It's amazing—I feel like Gulliver. The attention is wonderful—I realize that tea and food and kitten-love has made me feel better. When I sit up the kittens move away in panic, backs arched, tails as stiff as loo brushes.

'Thanks, Louie,' I say gratefully.

'No problem.'

I feel I owe her an explanation: 'There was a bit of a barney at home this morning.'

For some reason I am ashamed to tell her that Seth hit me, instead I tell her all about the party and Leo spiking Faye's drinks. Then I remember again about not turning up and I mumble an apology.

'Doesn't matter,' Louie says with a grin. 'It was just a shame you missed it. I had a brilliant time. The young 'uns were out of the sett and playing. I wish I had a camera or something. I'll take you up there when you're feeling better. Look, you have a bit of a sleep. I got to go and milk the goats but you stay here as long as you want to. I might see you later.'

Blue wakes immediately when she moves away and follows her dutifully out of the field. I lie down and the kittens return. They are tired now and curl themselves around me: one under my arm, another on my shoulder, and one under my chin, then we all go to sleep.

When I wake I know it is late in the day. The sun has moved and I can feel the rays gentle on my face. The kittens have disappeared. I realize I am ravenously hungry again. Before I leave I fold up the feed sack and the tartan rug and leave them in the shed. I have noticed how tidy Louie is, despite the ramshackle appearance of the huts and stable everything inside is pin neat. After I have done this, I make my way down the field and Fred follows me again, blowing through his nostrils and touching my bare arm with his whiskery old nose.

The cottage is deserted. No sign of Faye. I am relieved

because the mirror in the bathroom shows me a face leached to the same washed-out pale yellow of my hair, with dirty grey smudges like old bruises under my eyes. First of all I shower and change my clothes, then I set off to walk around the lake.

When I return to the cottage the sun is setting and Seth's car is parked on the verge. Stopping at the back door, I take a deep breath and compose my face. Then I walk in. The kitchen is full of the most wonderful aroma of garlic and onions. Honestly, I could dribble like Blue the instant I smell it. My mother and Seth are sitting at the table, holding hands and drinking wine. Faye is busy at the stove and in the background music is playing. Everyone stares at me.

I say 'Hi!' and go over to the sink to wash my hands.

Sneaking a sideways glance at Faye as I say: 'What's for supper? Smells good . . . '

Seth and my mother both start talking together. They are like Tweedledum and Tweedledee: 'Why didn't you explain . . . Why did you pretend . . . Inconsiderate . . . worried sick . . . A real pain . . . Can't be trusted . . . ' A torrent of accusation and recrimination. There is a basket of French bread on the table. I tear a hunk from the nearest loaf and stuff it into my mouth because I have no intention of replying.

'Well—here he is! And he looks fine! So there's no problem,' Faye says soothingly. Smiling at me she adds: 'It's seafood paella for supper. I hope you like it?' I look up at her and nod my head happily.

Seth opens his mouth to begin again but Faye gets in first: 'How did your last day of filming go, Pop? Did you get it all in the can?' Our eyes meet and she gives me a little grin.

Seth is like one of Pavlov's dogs. And now he has been thrown a morsel he can't ignore. You only have to mention his work and he immediately forgets everything else.

Now he starts telling us about the problems of open air shoots near water. My mother sits enraptured and Faye is busy at the stove. I just eat bread and think what a complete prat he is. It seems a strange kind of job for a grown man to do, spending his life pretending to be someone else.

It strikes me that I could maybe write a ghost story about an actor who gets taken over by his character. I am lost in this world to the extent that I don't hear Faye saying my name. Finally she touches my shoulder and I jump as if she has thumped me.

'Here's your supper, Alexander. Are you all right?'

'Perfectly. I was just thinking . . . ' I say, beginning to eat.

'What were you thinking about?' my mother asks, with a worried frown.

'About writing something for the school magazine. There's a short story competition,' I mumble.

'Well, that would be lovely,' she says, and I see a relieved look pass between her and Seth. 'I think Yorkshire is very inspirational. Just look at all the writers who have sprung from here.'

'Yes . . . ' I say pointedly. 'Who exactly were you thinking of?'

I see her eyes shift uneasily. 'Well, the Brontës . . . '

'Yes, who else?' I question again.

'There were three of them . . . ' she adds a little lamely.

'Very good!' I scoff.

'There must be some others, Alexander. Don't tease. Tell us?' Faye says quickly, trying to be a peacemaker.

'Well, there was J. B. Priestley from Bradford. John Braine, Stan Barstow, Keith Waterhouse, and Jilly Cooper.' I shoot a glance at my mother and add, 'To name but a few.'

There is an uneasy silence. Then Faye says: 'I think Yorkshire is beautiful—and so unspoilt. There is wonderful wildlife here. Alexander's friend, Louie, is going to show us a badger sett.' I know she is only trying to make conversation but I shoot her a warning look.

'That will be nice,' my mother says. 'I don't think I've ever seen a badger.'

'She only said she might show us. It isn't definite,' I say in a surly voice. And Faye shoots me an anguished look, uncertain what she has said or done wrong.

After we have finished eating my mother and Seth leave for the pub. I flop down in the chair next to the stove and watch Faye washing up. 'Do you want me to dry?' I ask.

'OK,' she grins, and throws the tea towel over to me. When we have finished she asks me if I want a coffee. I don't—but I say 'yes', just because it's so lovely to have her fussing around me.

We take our coffee into the sitting-room and switch on the TV. Faye touches my arm. 'Seth is really sorry about coming on so strong with you about the party.'

'Doesn't matter . . . ' I mumble.

'What I don't understand, Alexander, is why *you* didn't tell him what happened. He has a really bad temper, didn't you know?'

'Thanks for the warning.'

'Why didn't you just explain?'

She is staring at me with a perplexed look on her face, waiting for me to speak. What can I say to her? How do you tell someone they are so special, and what you feel for them is so intense, that you can't talk about them? It sounds too crazy to be true.

Finally I just mutter: 'I didn't want to.'

'Did you feel you had to protect me? Did you think I might get into trouble for getting drunk? It was very brave of you, Alexander. But I was worried sick about you. I spent all day looking around Barrowgate and Yarham for you.'

Words fail me. I feel really strung out. I don't know

whether to sit next to her on the settee or not. If I'm honest I would like to put my arms around her, hold her close, and kiss her a couple of times. But I have more chance of sprouting wings and flying than this happening.

Instead I sit slumped in one of the old armchairs, watching this nature programme on the TV, while Faye sits curled up on the settee with her feet tucked neatly under her. And I don't want to watch the dolphins on the screen, I want to look at her.

Eventually I lean back and close my eyes. I feel as if I might explode if I don't touch Faye, but then again, I might explode if I do. When I feel her touch on my hand I think I'm imagining it.

'Alexander. Are you OK? You're nearly asleep.' She is leaning over me, her hair is almost touching my face. I look up at her and smile.

'Honestly. I'm fine. It's just been a long day.'

'Are you sure you are OK?' She is frowning and I reach up and rub my first finger across the little bridge of skin between her dark arched brows.

'Don't frown, you'll get wrinkles,' I say, and she pats my hand away and laughs.

'I don't care about that, I'm worried about you.' She sits down on the floor next to my chair and takes hold of my hand. 'Seth didn't treat you fairly. I can understand if you are sore with him.'

'It doesn't matter,' I say, and really mean it. Nothing matters now she is holding my hand. When I was in the fourth year I wrote quite a few poems. It was after we studied the war poets: Owen, Brooke, and Sassoon. I got inspired and wrote about being frightened and dying but they were just copies—nothing real.

Now I feel there is something I need to put down in words. There is such a contradiction in me about everything: love, hate, despair, and hope are all mixed up in my head. I can't tell Faye how I feel because I don't understand it myself. I don't recognize these feelings which are filling me up: all I know is that I am like a brimming cup, one more drop and I might lose it.

'Tell me about America. What's it like?'

The most incredible thing happens. She leans against the chair and rests her head against me. I can feel her hair tickling my hand and I daren't move a muscle. So I keep still the way you would if a wonderful jungle creature had come out from the wild and sat next to you—scared to breathe in case it makes her move away.

She talks, softly and soothingly, about the States: about her home, her school, her friends. Sometimes she stops and I have to prompt her, but most of the time the words just flow. I keep asking questions until I know all about it: the ranch style houses, the straight roads, even the names of the exotic trees in the gardens, Royal palms and gumbo limbos. I want to know everything about her life there. Even what kind of biscuits she likes. Finally I am transported, no longer sitting in a dusty sitting-room in Yorkshire on a cool summer evening, but with her at the Gulf of Mexico, on a white sand beach where the pelicans fly.

'How can you bear to leave it and come here?' I ask, hungry as only dwellers of cold climates can be for sun, sand, and sea.

She laughs up at me: 'It gets real hot in the summer. Even Florida folk find it a little warm. Christmas time is nice for Europeans. Maybe you could visit?'

Closing my eyes I feign sleep. 'Yes . . . possibly,' I murmur.

'I like England. I hope Pop will let me stay with him. I know you two haven't hit it off, but he is an OK guy. Really . . . ' Her voice sounds anxious. Opening one eye I squint down at her.

'Really?' I echo mockingly. 'Tell me about it tomorrow. I don't feel in the mood tonight.'

'Alexander, I know this is asking a lot, but do you

think, please, you could try to be friends with him, even after what happened today?'

'Of course. No sooner said than done.'

'No. I mean it. You see I'm very fond of Diane already. She's the first woman he's dated who I've truly liked. And she treats me like a friend already. I really want things to work out for them and if . . . '

'OK, Faye. I get the picture.' My tone is bitter and I can't hide it. 'You're all going to play happy families and I'm not to rock the boat.' The hurt look on her face makes me wince and I turn away from her.

'Isn't that what you want?' she asks quietly.

'Look,' I hiss. 'I don't care what they do. All I want is a quiet life. I don't want to be part of their family—I don't want to be part of any family. Most of the time I wish I'd been born a orphan.'

'Alexander? What is the matter?' she whispers.

Suddenly I wish I could tell her. For the first time in my life I really want to open my heart and let all the pain out. But the words just won't come.

'You just want everything to be perfect. And life isn't like that!' I rise to my feet and her hand drops away from me. I have spoilt it all, all that lovely closeness and her sitting next to me.

'Why are we arguing, Alexander? I didn't want this to happen. There is so much I don't understand about you.'

I could tell her that there are many things I don't understand about myself but it sounds pathetic.

'Look, we're not arguing. Not really . . . ' I pass a weary hand over my eyes. 'I want us to be friends,' I manage to blurt out. It sounds really naff—like we're at junior school or something.

'So do I, Alexander, more than anything,' she says. Her expression and tone are so earnest that I manage a smile.

'Look, tomorrow morning I'll take you down to Louie's place and show you the kittens,' I say desperately.

97

'Thank you, Alexander, that will be very nice,' she says quietly. She moves across to me and for one insane moment I think she is going to take me in her arms and kiss me. But she merely reaches up and touches the side of my face lightly with her finger tips. 'I hope you sleep well, Alexander. You look so tired,' she whispers.

'Thanks. Goodnight . . . ' I mumble, as I stumble away from her. It would have been so easy to put my arms around her and kiss her. I've seen it done dozens of times at the cinema and on TV. I wish I'd practised a bit harder with Teresa Crispin. I wish I wasn't a retard. I wish I knew if she had wanted me to kiss her. But if wishes could come true we would all be millionaires. So I just go to bed and read *Wuthering Heights*—my mood is just right for a bit of unrequited love and misery.

9

Louie is grooming Fred when we arrive. She is wearing cut down jeans shorts and a filthy white T-shirt because it's really hot today. She obviously isn't in a good mood and I wonder if it's because I have brought Faye with me. Faye too is wearing shorts: crisp red shorts, which contrast with her navy shirt and smooth brown legs, she is also wearing little blue shoes with clean white laces. She looks like a sailor.

I lean against the gate. Louie finishes brushing Fred's coat and comes over to speak to us. The contrast between the girls almost hurts me; there is Louie, with her stick-thin legs—so pale they are almost green—and her grimy baseball boots and mop of dreadlocks, standing opposite the immaculate Faye. I feel irrational irritation with both of them. Maybe that knock on the head has affected me more than I realize. I'm cross with Louie for looking so dreadful: yet I'm also annoyed with Faye for looking so sparkling and neat.

'I hope you don't mind me coming down with Alexander?' Faye asks with her unfailing courtesy.

'No, but mind you don't get mucky,' Louie says, curling her lip slightly in what passes muster as a smile.

'I wondered if you'd like to come and have some lunch with us after we've seen the animals,' Faye says.

'You what?' Louie replies irritably.

I feel like shouting at her: 'Lunch. Dinner. Brunch. Midday meal. You know—the meal which most people have in the middle of the day.'

Instead I just sigh and Faye says quickly, 'It's just salad and bread. If you prefer I could pack it up and we could have a picnic.'

'Lunch? Oh, all right. Sorry. I'm just tired—I was up late.' Louie scowls at me as if it's my fault she hasn't understood.

'Did you go to see the badgers?' Faye asks politely.

'Who told you about them?' Louie snaps. 'I don't want word getting out. The last lot got baited and killed. I haven't told anybody about these and I make sure no one sees me go there.' She is so fierce I intervene.

'We won't tell anyone, Louie. It's OK. We came down to see the kittens.'

'Come on then,' Louie says, opening the gate. 'Don't mind Fred. He won't hurt you,' she says to Faye. 'And you've already met Blue.'

'Hi, Blue,' Faye says, bending down to pat Blue's head. 'Oh what a cute baby,' she adds, putting her arms around Fred's neck and hugging him. He, as if replying to this, lifts his head and neighs. Louie laughs.

'I can see you like horses. And Fred likes you,' she says with approval. 'Do you ride?'

'Sure thing,' Faye says, running her hands over Fred's neck. 'I have an uncle and cousins in Montana. I try to visit when they're herding steers. I love a week in the saddle.'

'You lucky thing,' Louie says enviously. 'A real cowgirl. That would be the life for me.' They are walking in step, with Blue trotting between them; suddenly deep in discussion talking saddles and branding and things I know nothing about. Me and Fred trail behind, both forgotten.

'Poor old boy,' I say, looking at his wonky old legs and drooping hind quarters. 'They're lusting after pintos and palominos and guys in leather trousers. You and me are right out with the bloody washing.' I feel unreasonably jealous of the male cousins in Montana galloping around on their horses being macho with branding irons and lassoes.

Faye goes crazy over the kittens. 'Louie, they are beautiful. Back home these would sell for a fortune. They've authentic wildcat markings. What's the mother like?'

'Well, she's an old farm tabby. I have wondered about the tom. I never seen him. And I go up there at night when you think he'd be around.'

'Where do you go?' I ask, suddenly intrigued by Louie's nocturnal wanderings.

She ignores me and carries on talking to Faye: 'I reckon the groom at the big house leaves the kittens here when he's been told to drown them. He's a smashing bloke and a bit soft hearted. He kept a kitten a few years ago and it looks like these. All stripes and spotted tummies.' Louie turns one of the kittens over and it tries to bite her hand. 'I'll tell you something strange, as well. They're not afraid of water.'

'Oh how exciting! Do you think the tom could be a Scottish wildcat?' Faye asks breathlessly. 'We aren't far from the Scottish borders, are we? And they do roam when they're looking for a new territory.'

'People say we had wildcats here at the turn of the century. I suppose there might be a few left,' Louie adds.

'Well,' I say with a grin. 'If there are any wildcats, or Neanderthals, left in Yorkshire then Gouthgill would be the perfect place to hide away.'

'What do you do with them when they're old enough to move on?' Faye asks, picking up each kitten in turn and stroking it.

'Sometimes I give them to the pet shop. Or I put a postcard in the window of the paper shop in Yarham and take them round to people's houses,' Louie says. 'I don't like the man in the pet shop, so I try to find them homes myself if I can.'

'Why don't you advertise them in the *Yorkshire Post*.

''Wildcat kittens. Ten pounds to good homes only'',' Faye suggests.

'Ten pounds!' Louie stutters. 'No one will pay that for a kitten.'

'Sure thing, they would. These kittens are beautiful and very unusual. And if people pay a reasonable amount for something they value it more. Look how folks cherish Siamese. And you . . . ' she picks up one of the kittens and kisses its nose, 'are much more beautiful than a Siamese.'

'Can't do it, we haven't got a phone . . . ' Louie admits glumly.

'We could do it, couldn't we, Alexander?' Faye turns to me, her eyes shining.

'Yes, of course we could. And we could show them the kittens at the house.'

'Oh, that would be OK. Couldn't do with folks traipsing down here,' Louie says with relief.

'Good, that's settled,' Faye says with satisfaction. 'Now shall we go and have some lunch?'

'Yeah. Great!' Louie says with more enthusiasm. 'And tomorrow night, if you like, I'll take you to see the badgers.'

'Oh yes, please,' Faye says happily.

I wait until Louie is busy tying up the gate with orange string before I ask the question: 'Louie, why do you go up to the big house at night?' She jumps guiltily and turns to face me like a terrier which has been cornered.

'Who says I go up there at night?'

'You did,' I say with a small smile. 'So what do you do?'

Louie gives me this really hard look, her small nut brown face is tight with temper as she says: 'I go nicking. Is that what you want to know?'

'Nicking?' Faye says bemused.

'Yeah. Pinching. Stealing. Taking stuff that isn't mine. What do you call it over in America?' Louie asks in an affronted tone.

'But, Louie, why do you do it? And what do you take?'
Faye asks, concerned.

'I take oats, pony nuts, hay, and corn for the pheasants.
I take a rucksack and fill it. Then I come home on my
bike. I can only go when the moonlight's right and I can't
take too much or they might start to notice. I have a couple
of other places I go. Farms where there's hay and oats in
the barns. But mostly I go to the big house. His lordship is
so rich . . . I mean it's not like stealing from poor people,
or folks who can't afford it.' Louie gives us both a
searching look. 'But if you don't want me to come and
have lunch with you, I don't mind.'

'It doesn't bother me . . . Karl Marx called it
redistribution of wealth,' I say with a grin. I give Faye an
enquiring look. She is looking worried.

'But what happens if you get caught?'

Louie laughs, she seems relieved that we are taking it
so well. 'I'll worry about that if the time ever comes.'

We have a brilliant time together and are out in the fresh
air all day. So I don't understand why I don't sleep that
night. But I have always suffered from insomnia—it
seems to be a habit I can't kick.

When I wake up I know it is late, because my bedroom
is hot and stuffy and the sun is beaming through the
window. On my bedside table is a filmy mug of coffee. It
tastes disgusting but I drink it anyway. When I go down
to the bathroom for a shower I hear the radio playing
downstairs and the buzz of the Hoover. What I really long
for is the smell of bacon cooking and coffee percolating.
I'm so hungry my stomach hurts. I also have this irritable
feeling that I've missed the best of the day, that everyone
else in the world has been doing something interesting
while I have been asleep.

In the kitchen a box of cornflakes and a bowl have been
left on the table for me. I pour out a great mound of cereal

and start eating. Then halfway through I realize I need a drink and get up to fill the kettle.

'I didn't realize you were up. I'll make coffee. How you doing? I came up earlier but you were fast asleep.' Faye's voice is kind, but it does little to ease my ill humour. 'I've phoned the *Yorkshire Post* and placed an advert for the kittens,' she adds.

'How did you do that?' I ask, through a mouthful of milk and cereal.

'I used my credit card. It'll go into the paper tomorrow morning. I hope we get lots of calls.' She hands me a cup of coffee. 'Would you like some toast? Or is it too late? It's nearly lunch time.'

'I know what time it is,' I say ungraciously. 'And I thought Americans ate all day. Didn't you lot invent brunch?'

'Hey,' she says with a grin. 'You can't be a grouch if you sleep until eleven.' She goes back to her hoovering and leaves me to my breakfast. The Hoover is old enough to be in a museum and because of the noise it makes we don't hear a car pull up outside.

The first inkling I get that we have a visitor is when I see a figure walking past the kitchen window and a female voice shouts: 'Cooee. Anyone at home?' Then the back door, which is ajar, is pushed open.

I sit at the table and stare. This is odd behaviour. No one in London would dream of walking into a house uninvited. But there in front of me stands a girl of about Faye's age, who is looking around the immaculate kitchen with a satisfied proprietorial air. This girl has shoulder-length blonde hair and a long-jawed intelligent face. I imagine that she will eventually become a doctor or a judge, or possibly a missionary—and God help the criminals or heathens when she does.

'Hello there,' she says enthusiastically. 'I don't think we met at the party. I'm Octavia Stanton.' When I look at her blankly she adds: 'Leo's sister.'

'Oh well, never mind. We all have our cross to bear in this life.' I reach for my mug of coffee and rise to my feet.

'Actually, I came to see Faye. Is she about?' Octavia gives me a smile which doesn't reach her eyes.

'She's next door in her other incarnation . . . ' Octavia looks at me blankly. 'Cleaning lady. I'll just get her,' I add, with a grimace of a smile.

I had planned to call Faye and then escape upstairs, but Faye comes into the kitchen, pushing the Hoover in front of her, and blocks the doorway.

'Hi! How you doing?' she calls cheerfully.

'Oh, it's super to see you again!' Octavia says with heartfelt relief, presumably because Faye's arrival means she doesn't have to be alone with me any longer. 'Leo asked me to come as his messenger. He ought to get down on his knees and grovel for being such an awful twit! He says he's very, very sorry and will you please forgive him?' Octavia pulls a comic face and Faye laughs. They don't appear to notice my scowl.

'He's a complete fool!' I say angrily. 'I hope he realizes how dangerous it is to give people alcohol without them knowing. He must be completely stupid!'

'Oh, come on,' Octavia says haughtily. 'He only gave her a tiddly little bit. He said the fruit cup was just too pissy for words without a shot of vodka in it.' She turns back to Faye and ignores me. 'Anyway, Faye, he says he really is truly sorry. He didn't realize you had awful jet lag or he wouldn't have pepped up your drink. Honestly he wouldn't! Anyway, he's riding at a gymkhana this afternoon and he said if you would like to come with us, it would be super to have you.'

'I bet it would,' I mutter.

'Well, I don't know. I kinda . . . ' Faye begins, darting an anxious look in my direction.

'Oh, please, do come! It would be so lovely. There's quite a crowd of us going. Pa has lent us the Range Rover so we can all squash in. There are tons of people who are dying to meet you—they will all be there. Do say you will, please!'

Octavia is so gushy, I can see that it has really disconcerted Faye.

'Well, I've never been to a gymkhana before . . . It would be cool . . . ' she starts to say.

Breaking in rudely, like a child who wants to be noticed, I say mockingly: 'Never been to a gymkhana, my dear girl! You simply haven't lived!'

'Well, OK then. Thanks for the invitation, that's swell. What time?' Faye says uncertainly.

Octavia is marching towards the door—her business accomplished. 'We'll fetch you at one o'clock. We've a picnic planned so don't eat lunch beforehand.'

'We'll be ready, won't we, Alexander?' Faye says nervously, shooting me a pleading look.

'I'm not going!' I say loudly.

Octavia turns at the door and gives me a cool smile: 'Oh, do come. It would be nice,' she says without enthusiasm.

'Oh please, Alexander!' Faye says. She sounds genuinely upset but I will not budge.

'No!' I say with a scowl.

'Oh well, another time, maybe,' Octavia says to me with icy indifference. 'See you at one o'clock, Faye. Tat-ta!'

After she has left I move across and shut the back door with a bang. 'That stupid girl must have been born in a barn. She walks in without knocking and then leaves the door open!'

'Alexander . . . ' Faye says pleadingly. 'Please don't be so angry. Come with us this afternoon—it'll be fun. We might end up being friends with the Stantons.'

'Friends with the Stantons!' I shout. 'You must be bloody joking.'

'Why not?' Her voice is dangerously quiet. 'Why not, Alexander?'

'Because they're not my sort of people . . . ' I say stubbornly.

'You British are just so snobbish!' Faye says ruefully. 'How do you know whether they're your sort of people until you get to know them?'

'I would have thought you'd got to know Leo well enough by now . . . ' I say sulkily.

'Oh, Alexander!' She gives this embarrassed little laugh and wrinkles her nose at me. 'I had a few drinks with the guy, a couple of dances. We talked a bit, that's all. I don't know what he's like . . . And it *is* generous of them to invite us. After the way we left their party I think it's kind of nice they still want to know us.'

'They invited you. I don't think I was included in it.'

'Alexander. This is just childish nonsense. Of course you were invited. Please come.'

'You don't have to go. You could phone and make an excuse.' I turn away from her because I am scared she will see the longing in my eyes. I want her to say she never wants to see Leo again for as long as she lives.

'Oh, Alexander,' she says sadly. 'I couldn't do that. It would be so impolite. I've said I'll go.'

'Please yourself,' I say bitterly, turning my back on her and piling my bowl and mug into the sink. 'But don't come crying to me if you make a complete fool of yourself with Leo Stanton. He's obviously after only one thing. I'm surprised you can't see that. Or maybe . . . ' I pause, my voice low and cruel. 'Maybe that's what you want!'

She comes across and pulls at my arm so I have to face her. For the first time since we met I see temper in her eyes.

'What exactly are you suggesting, Alexander?'

'Well, you *are* on the rebound from Erik, aren't you?' I say maliciously. The sight of her anger has pleased me, because it proves I can generate some kind of emotion in her. I'd rather she hated me than was just indifferent.

'Which generally means girls fall into bed with the first bloke who comes along,' I add airily, as if I'm a man of the world and know all about it.

Her hand cracks across my face like a whiplash. It makes me take a step back and I bang my spine against the rim of the sink. I wince with pain, but I'm too startled to say or do anything else.

Faye stands and stares at me with this awful twisted expression on her face as if she's in agony. 'Alexander . . . ' she whispers and her voice is breaking. Then I see her chin begin to wobble and her eyes fill with tears. 'Alexander. I'm sorry . . . ' She tries to put her arms around me, but I push her away.

'Just leave me alone!' I shout. 'I don't want anything to do with you. Move in with the Stantons if that's what you want. Be a complete slag and snog Leo until you're senseless for all I care.'

'Alexander! Don't say that,' she screams at me, as if I've put a voodoo curse on her or something awful.

I march out of the kitchen and up the stairs and all the time she is hanging on to my arm, trying to talk to me, but I shake her off as if she is a rather disgusting insect. I have to push her away quite hard to get my door shut and locked. First she rattles the door handle, then she talks to me: quietly at first, then louder, then shouting. But I sit on the bed, staring into space, ignoring her.

There are words I would like to shout at her: whore, slapper, tart . . . that kind of thing. But when I open my mouth nothing comes out. All I can think about is Leo and her dancing together at the party and the way he touched her. And now she is going out with him. He hasn't even bothered to ask her himself, but sent his stupid sister as a messenger. That takes some confidence. He must be very sure she would say yes. And Faye is just so stupid, so gullible. I feel crazy with jealousy, and angry too. I have taken her down to Louie's—I have shared everything with her. And now she is going off with Leo Stanton. I feel betrayed. I want so much to hurt her, but it takes me a while to work out how to do it.

Finally, I get my sax out of the case and start playing. Slowly, with as much melancholy as I can manage, I play all the saddest tunes I know: 'Memories' from *Cats*, 'Danny Boy' and 'Scarborough Fair'. Whenever there is a pause in the music I hear her voice wailing like a banshee outside the door pleading with me to open it.

For a little while, carried along on a high tide of temper, it makes me feel incredibly good to know she is hurting as much as me. But then I start to feel sad, the music and the sound of her sobbing gets to me. I know she is crying hard. I know her face is wet and that my mouth could slide across her cheeks and forehead . . . that I could touch her eyebrows and eyelashes with my lips and taste the salt of her tears.

Suddenly I very much want to comfort her . . . But I can't open the door and let her in. I'm scared to see what I've done. I can't bring myself to look at her with tears and snot running down her face and know that I've caused all that misery.

In a moment of complete self-loathing I realize that if I was a mature cool kind of guy I could have pretended I didn't care—and worked out a strategy to get her away from Leo. Now I've blown it. Despair at my own stupidity makes me carry on playing. The mournful notes of the sax rise through the window and drift along the curve of the lake and down to the bottom of the valley, until at last Faye is silent.

When I finally stop playing my lips are puckered and numb. And in some perverted way I'm glad to have a physical pain to ride pillion with the ache in my heart. I feel sick and bruised inside; dizzy with the terrible fear that I've killed something precious, that Faye and I will never be friends again and I am responsible.

Louie looks at me and pulls a face: 'What's the matter with you? You look as if you've won the lottery and lost the ticket.' I hadn't thought she would notice my pale miserable face so I haven't thought of an excuse.

'I've got a headache,' I say quickly. 'I suffer with hay fever.'

'Everyone's off it today. Old Fred won't eat his fodder. He's nothing but a bag of bones. I need to feed him up.' Louie chews at her lip for a moment, then she adds: 'Tell you what, let's go and see the badgers tonight. That'll cheer us up.'

'Yeah—great,' I say, without too much enthusiasm.

'Will Faye come too?' Louie asks.

'No.'

'You two had a row?'

'No,' I say quickly. 'Well, sort of—she's gone out with the Stantons. Don't know what time she'll be back.'

Louie doesn't often look straight at you. She has a funny habit of ducking her head when she talks to you. But suddenly I find myself, unwillingly, looking into her clear, vivid blue eyes. Her slightly cross-eyed, cat-like gaze is mesmerizing and I can't look away.

'That's what's given you the hump,' she says, shrugging her shoulders.

'That and the hay fever,' I say. 'I'll just help you get the kittens sold and then I'm going back to London—for definite.'

'Rather you than me. I hate cities,' Louie says. 'Drives me mad when we visit my Nan in Leeds. Don't know how people put up with the pong from all those cars and buses. Still, each to his own. Come on,' she chivvies me gruffly. 'You look all in. Go and have a kip under the tree.'

I didn't know I was tired, but I go to sleep immediately. When I wake the sun has set and dusk is settling. There is a wonderful smell of hot meat and pastry in the air as Louie appears with a plate of pie and peas and a huge mug of tea.

'Brought you some supper.'

'Thanks,' I say gratefully. 'I feel better now. I was tired. How did you know?''

'I'm good with animals,' Louie says with a grin. 'When you've had that we'll have to go and get set up. Have to be there early and keep dead quiet if you want to see the badgers. You got a jumper or something? Gets cold sitting under a bush in the middle of the woods.'

'I'll get one from the cottage when we go past.'

'Don't say anything about seeing the badgers, will you? I don't want word getting out,' Louie says anxiously.

The cottage is deserted, there is a note on the table saying they have gone to the pub and my dinner is in the fridge—another salad. I grab a packet of chocolate biscuits from the larder and a jumper from my room and rejoin Louie.

We walk along the far side of the lake where there is a rough cart track instead of a road. The over-hanging trees make it dark, if I wasn't with Louie and Blue I wouldn't be too happy about being there. It's not scary like the city, it's frightening like nothing I've ever experienced before; a combination of silence, darkness, and loneliness. Now I know why writers of fairy tales and myths portray woods and forests as full of danger.

At the end of the lake the cart track peters out. 'This is the last place we can talk or make a noise,' Louie says in a whisper. I hadn't thought we'd been making much noise, only eating biscuits and walking, but I realize that greater stealth is needed now. We finish the last three biscuits between us. 'I've two different hides, depending on which way the wind is blowing. We have to stay down wind of them or they'll scent us. Once we're in position I'll pinch your arm. After that you have to stay as still as you can . . . really quiet. Will the hay fever make you sneeze?'

'Oh no,' I whisper quickly.

'That's a relief!' Louie says mockingly, and I wish I

hadn't been so stupid as to lie to her. Then she adds more kindly: 'Is there anything you want to ask before we go in?'

'No, I don't think so.'

I'm rather wishing I hadn't come. My legs are aching from the long walk and the dankness of the wood is oppressive. The next bit is awful because we have to move up the hill picking our way between the trees. The evening air is damp on my face and the air is heavy and still, laden with the smell of peaty soil and growing things.

Brambles and branches snatch at my clothes with spiteful fingers. It's like being barracked in the playground by a gang of bullies. And because I am so tall, I have to duck under all the low hanging branches and that makes my back ache.

We come upon the clearing quite unexpectedly. One second we're in the thick of the trees, moving cautiously over the uneven ground, and then suddenly we're in a space with the night sky like a huge dark-blue ceiling above our heads. I raise my head and breathe the fresh air gratefully. The white circle of the moon is just rising above the dark shadow of the trees and beneath it hangs the evening star, shining like one of the diamonds in Faye's earrings.

Louie signals to me to follow her. Then she gets me settled on an old wooden box behind a screen of branches and pinches my arm firmly. I sit and stare into the centre of the clearing.

I'd never realized before how very difficult it is to keep still. Once I am trapped on my box I discover that I'm moving all the time, scratching, sniffing, shifting my shoulders around, tapping my feet. Trying not to move is torture. To make it worse I am aware of the shadowy form of Louie next to me, and she is as still and silent as one of the carved angels in the churchyard. And old Blue follows suit. He could be a crusader's dog immortalized in marble he is so quiet and unmoving, whereas I'm jiggling around like a demented puppet.

Even though I try to concentrate on the moonlight which has flooded the clearing I still fidget: I'm convinced all my unnecessary movements will stop the badgers from coming and grow increasingly depressed.

Then suddenly I sense Louie's excitement as something moves on the far side of the clearing—it's a snout, being lifted into the air, scenting the night, looking for danger. It disappears. I'm convinced that the badgers will not come out and it's all my fault.

But then there is a rustling and slowly into the clearing comes a badger. I'm so amazed by the sight of it that I nearly fall off my box. I have to make a conscious effort not to grab hold of Louie's arm and shout. Pressing my hands down onto my knees I steel myself not to move or make a sound. Then, after a few moments, there is more rustling and into the clearing tumbles a whole family of badgers. The moonlight illuminates them in a strange metallic way which increases the beauty of their black and white markings. It's as if we have all been transported to an alien world where there is no colour: just black and white and a million shades of silver.

I'd not realized badgers were so big. The adults are about the same as a medium-sized dog, made bigger by the distortion of the moon shadows. And, just for a moment, I'm nervous of them. Then my fear turns into a big ball of emotion that bounces around in my chest until I feel quite breathless. I watch the two adults begin to snuffle in the undergrowth while the three youngsters begin to play fight and roll around. They're like young humans, they want to mess about and have fun. I've never had a pet, or any animal I've been close to, but something strange happens to me as I watch the badgers. I feel an aching love for them, as if I'm connected to them by some invisible tie which binds us together.

It seems to pass in a flash. The waiting seemed like hours but the time they are in front of us seems only minutes. They play and feed and then wander off together into the undergrowth. When they have gone we also silently depart. I am so cramped from sitting on the box that I can hardly move and I stumble down the hill like an old man.

When we get down to the cart-track I look at my watch and am amazed at the hours which have passed.

'Louie,' I whisper. 'That was amazing. Thank you very much.'

'Yeah, they're great, aren't they? Tonight was perfect because the moon is bright and you could see them really well.' She sounds like a proud mother and I can understand that.

'How on earth did you find them?' I ask.

'I know what to look for. But I had to hunt for a long time to find this sett. There was one closer to the road but it got raided.'

'Why do people kill them? They are so beautiful.'

'Why do people shoot stags and hunt foxes? They do it for sport,' Louie says bitterly. 'The rich lot go on pheasant and grouse shoots and the roughs from the cities come out with their bull terriers and bait badgers. I'd like to put them all on a rocky island with no food and let them loose on each other. Anyway,' she says more cheerfully, 'I've been really careful about this sett. You're the only person I told about it and you haven't told anyone, have you?'

'Only Faye.'

'Well, she won't have told anyone, will she?' Louie asks.

'No.'

'Remind her when you see her. Don't tell anyone,' Louie reiterates.

'All right, yes I will.'

'You'll see her in the morning, won't you?' Louie asks suspiciously.

'I suppose so . . . ' I say miserably. I have this horrible feeling that Faye will never speak to me again and that the next time I see her she will look straight through me, her brown eyes hard and cold, her face bland and smooth.

'I promise I'll remind her not to talk about the badgers to anyone,' I say. I don't know if this is a promise to Louie or to myself, but it makes me feel a bit better. One way or the other I will have to speak to Faye now.

10

That night I dream of Faye. She is lost in the badger's wood and I can't find her, all I can hear is her voice crying. When I finally jerk awake I am sweating and my jaw is stiff from clenching my teeth. It's such a relief to be out of the dream that I race downstairs to see her, but the cottage is clean and tidy and empty. On the table is a polite note from Faye:

> *Dear Alexander,*
> *The phone hasn't stopped! We have lots of people coming to see the kittens this evening. I have gone shopping for cat litter and food so we can give the new owners a starter pack. I hope you had a nice evening. I didn't wake you because I know you were late. See you later.*
> *love,*
> *Faye*

Making myself some coffee and toast I reread the letter several times. There is no acrimony in her tone; I wonder if our row can be forgotten and if I can bury my jealousy and she her anger. I realize it's really childish of me to keep looking at the note and wondering if she puts *love Faye* to everyone she writes to. Eventually, irritated with myself, I fold the note up very small and put it in my jeans pocket. I wander out into the garden and realize from the height of the sun that it's nearly lunch time, so I grab some bread and go to find Louie.

The road down to the church is dappled in sunlight and I walk slowly, looking at the flowers in the hedgerows. There is an amazing variety: some are heavy and yellow, with clusters of blooms like clotted cream, while others are small and pink with ragged petals. I never knew weeds could be so pretty—in London we only get dandelions.

The goats are in the churchyard. I empty my pockets of the bread I have brought them and they butt me with their noses when all the food has gone. Laughing I hold out my hands to them. 'It's all gone, greedy girls. You'll have to make do with graveyard grass now.' When I turn around I find that Louie and Blue are standing right behind me.

Louie grins: 'I'm taking them up to the shed to milk them, want to learn?'

'What? To milk?'

'Yes, there's nothing to it. I bet they'll stand like little angels for you. They love you.'

'Oh, I'm so glad they love me,' I say, laughing. 'When I get back to London all I have to do is find a girlfriend who smells like a goat—then I'll be all right.'

'You don't need a girlfriend, stupid, when you've got Faye,' Louie says bluntly. 'And I don't know why you're always on about going back to London. You don't really want to—you know you like it here now.' She unties one of the ropes and hands it to me. 'Come on, make yourself useful, you can take Tinker. Have you kissed and made up with Faye, yet?' she asks with a sly grin.

'No. I haven't seen her. She's gone shopping to get things for the kittens. There's lots of people coming this evening. If it works well we could try to sell the puppies as well.' I scuffle my feet. I want to ask Louie if she really believes that Faye likes me but I'm too embarrassed.

'We'll have to take them around by the road. There's hogweed next to the path; I don't want 'em grabbing a mouthful.'

As we walk along the main road a car pulls up. I don't take too much notice at first because Snowy has found some blue flowers in the ditch and is trying to eat them. I am pulling at her halter, pleading with her to give over.

Then I hear a supercilious voice say: 'Hey there, Alex! Do you know where Faye is? I've been up to the cottage and there's no sign of her.'

Yanking Snowy out of the ditch I haul her up onto the road so that she is standing next to me. 'Stay there, you monster,' I hiss.

'I say how awfully clever!' the voice continues. 'Are you teaching her to walk to heel?' Leo Stanton laughs at his own joke.

'Actually we're going to run away and join a circus.'

Leo looks at me and laughs again: 'Do you know where Faye is by any chance?'

'No.'

'Do you know when she'll be back?'

'No.'

'Very helpful,' he says mockingly. 'Maybe I should have asked the goat.'

'Good idea. She's got a higher IQ than most people in the village,' I retort.

'I say, Alex. Tell Faye I'll ring her this evening. Or if she wants to give me a bell I'll be at home.'

Before I can reply Snowy dives into the ditch again, taking me with her, so all I hear is the roar of an engine as Leo Stanton drives off in his green sports car.

Louie looks at my furious face and says: 'Come on, Alex. I'll teach you how to milk a goat. I bet you that's something old Snobby Stanton can't do.'

I soon find out that milking goats isn't going to be one of my skills either. Snowy, or Tinker, as Louie calls her, is an absolute pig to milk. She dances around and turns her head to look at me with disapproval and disappointment as I fumble around.

Louie comes and shows me again: 'Squeeze and pull, squeeze and pull,' she chants rhythmically, and the milk shoots in a bluish white stream into the bucket with a pleasing plonking sound. But when I try it there is nothing but a dribble and Snowy moving restlessly.

'Come on,' Louie encourages. 'Keep trying. Lean your head against her and calm down. You're too tense. Think about something else.'

All I can think about is Leo Stanton and his car. He will be phoning Faye, asking her out, and he can take her anywhere: to a pub or a restaurant . . . for a ride in the country . . . to a lover's lane where he can take her in his arms in the soft sweet darkness of the night . . .

Snowy briskly side-steps away from me and kicks the bucket over. The small amount of milk in the bottom of the pail disappears into the earth floor of the shed.

'Gawd, I'm sorry, Louie,' I say miserably.

Louie rolls her eyes to heaven and says: 'You can't give up, it's not difficult.' She gets hold of Snowy's halter and says to her affectionately: 'Come on, misery-guts.'

After she has given the goat some hay to eat, I settle down on the stool again and try to think of something pleasant. Firstly I imagine Faye shopping, then I speculate on what she is wearing. Finally I think about her note and try to visualize her writing it. Closing my eyes I can see her inside my mind, bent over the kitchen table, her hair falling forward.

Suddenly I am jolted into reality by the sound of rain—then I realize the noise is milk cascading into the bucket. My hands are moving with tiny movements, but it's enough. Snowy is standing patiently with a long-suffering expression on her goaty face and the milk is gushing out.

'There, you see!' Louie says with satisfaction. 'You just had to relax—it all comes naturally.'

'I wish everything in life came as naturally as milking a goat,' I say, peering into the bucket when I have finished.

Louie laughs. 'Do you want to go and see the badgers again tonight? The weather is going to change and we may not have a good night for a while. You need moonlight and clear weather if you want to see them.'

'How do you know the weather's going to change?' I ask curiously.

Louie shrugs. 'I can just smell that it's going to rain,' she says. 'We might get a quick trip in tonight though, what do you say? Ask Faye if she wants to come.'

'OK. Shall I take the kittens back up with me?' I expect Louie to be upset about parting with them, or at least to say goodbye. But she finds a cardboard box and pops them in one by one without any sentiment at all.

'Aren't you sorry to see them go?' I ask curiously.

'It means less work, fewer mouths to feed. I shall miss them,' she says. 'But I need to get some medicine for Fred from the vet so I can do without kittens to worry about.'

'Is Fred ill?'

'He's really poorly. He's not long for this world,' Louie says abruptly, and she turns away quickly so I can't see her eyes. 'He was an old dinosaur when I got him—he can't go on forever.'

'How did you get him?' I ask gently.

'I went to the market with my father. He was buying stock for his lordship. Old Fred was the last lot. No one wanted him. The meat man had put in his bid but I upped it. I didn't have enough money so I asked the auctioneer for credit. He turned nasty but some of Dad's mates had a whip round and bought him for me.' Louie gives me a lop-sided grin. 'He's the best present I ever got.'

I swallow hard, remembering Fred's whiskery kisses, how he nudges my back when I walk across the field, and his big teeth and velvet lips when he takes carrots from my hand. 'Do lots of old horses go to the meat man?' I ask gruffly.

'Yes, that's where they go, back into the food chain. No one wants old horses—they eat too much.' She looks at me and grins. 'It's just as well they don't get rid of humans who eat too much. You and me'd be for the chop.'

What with Louie talking about Fred dying, and Leo Stanton sniffing around Faye like some old tom cat, I feel really depressed as I walk up the road with the box full of kittens. To make it worse the kittens go mad at being shut in the box. They make the most pitiful noises, little meows and high-pitched cries. They clamber up the side of the box, clinging with their razor-sharp claws, pressing their little pink noses against the holes we have made in the top. One tears at a hole, crying fiercely, and manages to get a paw through. It scratches at my hand when I cover the hole and I start to run because if I'm not careful I will have kittens all over the road.

Faye is waiting at the cottage. She has a litter tray and lots of newspaper down in the sitting-room. I dump the box and open it with relief. The kittens bolt away from me and the cardboard box as if we are instruments of torture. With fierce meows they claw their way up the back of the settee and one, braver than the others, scales the ancient velvet curtains.

'Get it down, it'll get dust poisoning,' I say, flopping down into a chair. Faye hands me a can of Coke and smiles sympathetically.

'We've got the first person arriving soon to look at them.'

'Well, I hope they have something strong to transport the little horrors. They can eat their way through cardboard. I thought I was going to lose them all.'

'Come on, cuties,' Faye says to the kittens, and one by one she collects them and shows them the litter tray and their food. By the time the first people arrive they seem quite civilized. I go into the kitchen and hide while all the people are in there choosing their kitten. I'm going to miss them dreadfully. And it will be worse when the puppies go because each day I get my favourite black and white pup out and give him a cuddle.

Eventually everyone leaves and Faye comes back into the kitchen. Curled in the crook of her elbow is the largest and boldest of the kittens, the one who climbed the curtains.

'Looks like we got one left over,' she says with a mischievous grin. She dumps the sleeping kitten onto my lap and begins to wash her hands. 'Seems we'll just have to keep him.'

'But what will Seth say? And what will happen when you go back to America?'

'Oh, Alexander! Don't worry! Let's just deal with one problem at a time. Now, what shall we call him?'

'I don't think—' I begin.

'How about Tiger?' she suggests. I assume she is joking but I when I look up I see that her face is serious.

'Yes, not the most original name but very nice,' I say carefully.

She grins at me. 'Well, he sure looks like a Tiger.'

Looking down at the vertical stripes on the kitten's back and the rings around its tiny tail I have to agree. 'Yes, I suppose he does. But it's just as well we aren't all named for our looks or there would be an awful lot of people called Spotty or Nerd. Speaking of which, Leo Stanton said he'd call you this evening.'

She laughs and begins to prepare supper. 'You know, Alexander, Leo really is a very sincere person. And I think that if you got to know him you would get on well together. You have a similar sense of humour.'

'The words sense of humour and Leo Stanton just don't seem to go together somehow,' I say wearily.

The kitten wakes and claws his way up my T-shirt. He settles on my shoulder like a parrot and begins to lick my cheek, I feel his rough sandpaper tongue moving up towards my ear. He smells of milk and cat biscuits. I am suddenly overwhelmed with happiness because Faye is keeping him.

'Don't go out with Leo tonight,' I say, suddenly full

of courage. 'Come and see the badgers with Louie and me.'

'Cool,' Faye says easily, as she begins chopping vegetables. Her face is turned away from me so I can't see her expression. I wish she would say she didn't want to go out with Leo Stanton anyway, but she doesn't. I will just have to be satisfied with her company for that evening—I can't expect more.

It seems impossible that Louie is right and it's going to rain: the air is warm, balmy, and flower-scented like a Mediterranean night. We shut Tiger in the attic with a litter tray and some food. He seems to be missing his brothers and sisters and has gone to sleep in the middle of my pillow as if desperate for closeness to some living thing.

Seth and my mother are working late so we have not told them about our new arrival. I feel that by the morning, when Tiger has spent the night at the cottage, he will be somehow established and they will not be able to turn him away.

As Faye and I walk down the road together I get this ridiculous fizz of joy, like sherbet exploding inside my chest. I want to sing or do a tap dance or something outrageous, just because I'm so happy to be walking next to Faye, and to know that I have her company for the whole evening.

Louie and Blue are waiting for us in the lane and we slip like shadows into the cool quiet of the wood. High above us an owl begins to hoot. It makes Faye jump. She is so close to me I feel her body quiver with shock.

It's hot work climbing up through the trees, the wood seems to resent our presence even more this evening, low-hanging branches and brambles seem to grab at us. It wouldn't take much imagination to believe that these spiteful nips and scratches are the fingers of vengeful ghosts. I begin to wish I'd never read *The Lord of the Rings*; I feel as if the trees are out to get me. Just before we reach the top of the hill there is an ominous grumble of thunder vibrating through the air, like giant footsteps in the sky.

Faye grabs hold of my hand and holds it tightly. I wish my palm wasn't so sweaty. I wish I wasn't so scared.

Louie stops and hisses at us. 'The storm is a few miles away. It might miss us altogether. If it doesn't I reckon we've about half an hour. Do you want to go on?'

'Yes,' Faye says.

I wish we could turn back. Now we are here I have a strange reluctance to go on to the clearing. I dread the thought of sitting on that hard wooden box and trying to keep still. Faye is sure to notice what a fidget I am and it seems such a trivial childish thing to suffer from. It is something which has always driven my mother mad. I doubt whether her constant nagging helped—it probably made it worse. Over the years, right from being a little boy, I seem to have been engulfed in endless tirades: 'Leave your nose alone! Alex—don't let those fingers wander! Alex—don't adjust your underwear in public. Alex—don't scratch. Take that paper clip out of your ear! Sit still—whatever is the matter with you?'

The matter with me is that my mother never wanted a grotty little boy with horrible habits. My mother wanted a little girl, sugar and spice and all things nice, and if it wasn't for me, she might have got what she wanted.

Tonight I don't get the chance to fidget. We have no sooner got settled on the box when a single heavy drop of rain lands on my forehead, like a big gob of spit thrown from the sky. I don't want to believe that it's going to rain because it's so lovely to have Faye sitting next to me. It's wonderful to feel the warm bareness of her arm pressing against mine and smell the lovely hot scent of her: perfume, sweat, and shampoo all mixed up together. Her hair is tickling my chin and, if I moved another inch, it would be so easy to press a kiss against her temple. I feel enveloped by her, as if her aura has moved around me, so I'm still and quiet and unbelievably happy. If it were possible I would sit here forever; nearly kissing her, feeling her warmth, smelling her scent. It's as if she's wrapped herself around my soul, like paper on a parcel, and I am contained and made whole. It can't bloody well rain and spoil it all!

I sit very still, hoping against hope that the rain will go away and leave us alone, trying to ignore the pitter patter of drips coming through the trees and the cold wetness falling on my face. Faye leans closer, her mouth so near to mine we are almost kissing.

'Alexander, honey. It's raining real hard.'

'Yes I know . . . '

'Do you want to go back?'

'No . . . '

Louie appears like some kind of ghoul next to us. She has wrapped an old feed sack around her shoulders to keep dry. 'Are you two going to sit there all night?' she says irritably. 'It's a waste of time. They won't bring the little 'uns out in a storm.'

'It's only a bit of rain . . . ' I hiss sullenly.

'Animals have got more sense than humans,' Louie says grimly. 'They don't like thunder and neither do I. Now shift yourselves—because I'm off. I want to check on old Fred.'

At that moment, from just above our heads, comes a monstrous belch of thunder, and the sky is lit up by a huge white light. It scares me witless. I grab hold of Faye and press her into my chest.

'It's OK, Alexander. I'm not afraid of thunderstorms,' she whispers.

If I was one of those 'new man' kind of guys who are confident about themselves I would admit, 'Well I am'. But I don't have the courage to confess to being scared.

It's easier going down the hill. The wood seems to speed us along, clearing a path through thickets and bramble patches as if pleased to see the back of us. Behind us the wood darkens, as if a door is being closed, as if we are being excluded, and I shiver with a mixture of cold and relief as we finally make it down to the cart track.

The rain is coming down in cold hard shards which hurt your skin when they hit you. Once we get to the lane Louie and Blue disappear without saying a word.

'I think she's worried about Fred,' Faye explains. In the dimness of the dark night I can see the pale shadow of her face and her hair, black and slicked down with water.

'Come on, let's get home,' I say, and I take hold of her hand and start to run. Almost instantly we find a pace which suits both of us. It's beautiful the way I shorten my stride and she lengthens hers so we can run together; we are like a horse and rider, or a windsurfer on the crest of a wave, together we make something perfect. This is the only time in my life I've run through the rain, getting absolutely soaked, and not minded. I feel as if I could run all night, run all the way to London, run my way into a new life. I almost want to say to her: 'Let's see how far we can go. Let's not stop until we are too tired to take one more step. Let's go and join the new age travellers for the summer . . . '

But I know it's an idiotic dream, fuelled by the exhilaration of running. I can't imagine Faye living in a tent for the summer, and as for me—I'd be lost without my CD player, my books, and three meals a day.

We fall in through the back door, breathless and laughing. I'm still holding her hand. I never want to let go of it. We both are shocked into silence. Seth and my mother are sitting at the table, they are sitting in silence, just doing nothing. It's like being faced with a judge and a jury. At any moment I expect Seth to find a black handkerchief, cover his head and give me a death sentence.

Faye drops my hand and I stand awkwardly, suddenly

bereft, like a child whose comfort blanket has been stolen.

'Hi there . . . ' Faye says hesitantly, her voice faint and breathy. And then, more strongly, 'What's the matter?'

Suddenly I am cold and I move gingerly over to the stove. My trainers squelch on the floor and I half expect my mother to tell me to take them off and not make a mess. But she is busy wiping her eyes, something has made her cry. I lean against the stove trying to catch my breath. I keep one eye on Seth. There is trouble in the air and I don't like it.

'What's the problem? Has someone shot the President?' I ask, and Seth winces.

'Your father phoned for you. He's called twice,' my mother says miserably. 'The baby has been born too early. It . . . she . . . ' she corrects herself quickly. 'She is very poorly in an incubator. They are going to christen her tomorrow. They want you to be there . . . ' She covers her face with her hands. This news seems to have really freaked her. It must be guilty conscience for all the horrible things she's said about Mandy.

'Your father says Mandy keeps asking for you and insists on waiting until you can get there,' Seth says. I don't reply. I don't really know what to say. I am still breathless from the running, still wrapped up in Faye. I can't think straight.

'Get changed and get your stuff together,' Seth says shortly. 'I'll drive you down.'

'What now?' I echo stupidly. All I can think is that I don't want to go. I don't want to leave Faye.

'Yes—now!' he snaps, as if I am a disobedient dog. When I think of the way Louie speaks to her animals it makes me sick to think that he uses this tone of voice with me—you'd think I was off the species list. I should think Louie would talk to a *frog* more nicely than Seth talks to me.

I try to catch Faye's eye, I want one look from her before I leave. But she is leaning over my mother, putting a protective arm around her, and my mother is crying into the comfort of Faye's shoulder. Faye doesn't even glance up at me. I daren't stand and stare at her for any longer. I am aware of Seth's hawkish gaze. Maybe it's just as well not to do or say anything in front of him. He is such a completely paranoid obsessive. I don't want to find I am banned from seeing her. Miserably, I slosh my way upstairs in my waterlogged shoes and begin to pack.

11

It is weird driving with Seth because he doesn't speak to me—not a single word until we have been driving for a couple of hours—then he suggests that I get into the back and try to sleep. I'm not tired but I move to get away from him. I keep asking myself how a charisma-free person like him managed to have a daughter like Faye. Maybe she was adopted—or his wife cheated on him.

Unexpectedly, once I am in the back of the car, I do sleep, and don't wake until we pull into a service area. Peering out I realize it's morning; the sun is just rising, filling the sky with a delicate milky pink—the colour you find sometimes inside a sea shell. Dawn has a completely different atmosphere to the rest of the day and it is so rare for me to be awake I want to notice all the subtle changes; thin rays of sunlight, dew on the grass, lack of traffic on the motorway. I move my cramped shoulders around, and rub the sleep from my eyes, trying to take it all in.

'You OK?' Seth asks, without looking at me.

'Yes, I'm fine.' I will not tell him that I feel rather sick. I bet Seth prides himself that he could cross the Atlantic in a bath tub and not take so much as an aspirin. He parks the car and I stagger out, gratefully breathing in the cool air.

'Thought we'd have breakfast and maybe a wash and brush up,' Seth says, stretching his arms above his head. 'It's too early to go to the hospital or call your father up. I could do with a coffee anyway.' He frowns at me, as if noticing my green pallor, and adds: 'You look as if you could do with something to eat. You OK, kid?'

I just nod and follow him into the service station. The deserted foyer is being vacuumed by two teenage zombies who have the vacant expression and lifeless eyes of people who have been awake all night. We move past them and head for the cafeteria: it smells of disinfectant and greasy bacon and my stomach heaves. Seth orders a full English breakfast with extra toast and a pot of coffee, but I just have tea and toast.

I watch him, as I play with my toast and sip the scalding grey tea, fascinated and repelled because he eats like a machine. He works with precision as he moves across the plate, like a combine harvester decimating a field of grain, big hands moving swiftly; cutting food, changing utensils, popping morsels into his mouth. The American way of eating has never before seemed so annoying.

'You done? I'm off to the men's room,' he says, finishing the last dregs of his coffee. I pour myself another cup of ghastly tea and stare into space wondering what the day ahead will hold. I'm not dreading it or anything— I'm just rather curious. It seems so odd that Mandy has asked for me.

'Are you going use the bathroom or something?' Seth's voice breaks into my reverie. 'I've got a rehearsal at noon. I need to make a move.' His hair is slicked back from his face with water and I can smell cologne and toothpaste hanging around him in a sickening cloud.

'All my gear's in the car,' I say lamely.

'They got toothbrushes and stuff in a machine in the john. You got a couple of pound coins?' With a sigh of irritation he reaches into his jeans pocket. 'Come on, Alex,' he says. 'I'll get a newspaper and meet you back at the car, but shift it, will you?'

I take his money reluctantly. My wallet is in my rucksack in the car so I have no alternative. Washing my face and cleaning my teeth does make me feel better and when I get into the car he gives a grunt of approval.

'You got enough cash for a couple of days in London?'

'Yes, thank you,' I say politely.

'Where are you going to stay?'

'I don't know, haven't thought about it yet. With my mate, Danny, if he hasn't gone on holiday.'

Seth clears his throat and says: 'Keep cool, won't you, Alex?'

'Is a heatwave predicted?' I question.

'You know what I mean, Alex! Your mother's had enough hassle to last her a lifetime—she doesn't need any more. She's doing swell in this new job and things are going good with us . . .' He gives me a knowing grin, just as if we are two buddies talking men's talk.

'Really?' I say icily.

'I'm crazy about her,' he says softly.

'Well! That is a relief, I'm sure. I had hoped that your intentions were entirely honourable.' I am becoming more English and proper with each moment that passes. By the time I get out of the car I may have turned into a reincarnation of Noël Coward.

'You see what I am trying to say, Alex? Just cool it while you're in London and don't get into any kind of trouble.'

'What kind of trouble had you in mind?' I query.

'You know, drugs . . . dope. You city kids are all into it. I know.'

'Are we?' My voice is sullen. I resent his pathetic attempt to talk down to me. Will he go back and report to my mother that we had a little tête-à-tête and he put me straight on the dangers of youthful living? Arrogant twat!

'Alex.' His voice is very low, very pleasant. 'What I'm trying to say is—if you do anything to upset your mother while you're away, you will have to answer to me.'

This is staggering! I only set eyes on this man a couple of weeks ago and now he's talking heavy stuff to me like he's my father. It's tempting to tell him that bedding my mother does not give him any kind of rights over me. But I hold my tongue because of Faye. Already I am desperate to get back to Yorkshire and see her. I can't afford to fall out with Seth, much as I would like to tell him to eff off. I sit in surly silence and do not answer.

'Do you love your mother at all?' he asks grimly and I am thrown by the unexpectedness of this question.

'Doesn't everyone love their mother?' I answer. This is getting boring.

'No,' Seth says. There is a pause while he overtakes a large lorry. 'Maybe you could use some therapy?' he suggests quietly.

'Would you mind stopping at the next service station?' I ask politely. 'I want the toilet.'

When he stops the car I grab my rucksack from the back. 'You can turn around and go back to Yorkshire. I can hitch the rest of the way.' My voice is calm and steely.

'No!' he says. He looks genuinely shocked, even a bit hurt. 'Alex, give me a break! I told your mother I would take you to your father's flat. I can't just leave you here!'

Without bothering to reply I just turn and walk away. I don't want to fight with him but neither can I sit in that car with him any longer.

Even though it takes me ages to hitch a ride into town, I get to my father's flat before he is up, and have to lean on the door bell for ages before he answers.

'Alex . . . you here already? Did you get an early train?' he mumbles, fiddling with the cord of his pyjama trousers and giving me a cross-eyed, sleep-befuddled look.

'I think you better let me in before you get arrested for indecent exposure,' I say, looking with disgust at his tousled hair and bare chest.

'Yeah, yes, come in. Sorry. I didn't think you'd be here so early.'

Holding his pyjamas up with one hand and scratching his head with the other he leads me into the sitting-room.

I almost gag when I walk in there. The room is foggy with the smell of beer and stale cigarette smoke.

'I'll make some coffee,' my father says. He disappears into the kitchen and I move across the room to open the windows as wide as they will go because the fug is making me feel really sick. In desperation I start emptying the brimming ash trays into the waste-paper basket.

The basket is already full of cig packets and beer cans, it smells awful, as if something rotten is lurking in the bottom. When I carry it into the kitchen my father is standing looking out of the narrow window. He has filled the kettle but forgotten to switch it on.

The kitchen is a pigsty even by my not very high standards. I can tell exactly how long Mandy has been away by the number of used plates on the table and the takeaway containers stacked on the work-top amongst the litter of coffee mugs and newspapers. There are no clean mugs in the cupboard and the dishwasher is full of foul plates and cups with mould growing in the bottom.

'Are you OK?' I ask, running hot water into the sink and putting a couple of mugs in to soak.

'Yes.' He runs his hands through his hair and turns to face me. 'I just haven't had much time and, as your mother was so fond of telling me, I'm not very domesticated.'

'I don't know about domesticated. You're not even bloody housetrained! What's Mandy going to say if she sees the place like this?' I ask.

'Look, just make me some coffee, please, Alex,' he says. 'I'm going to have a shower.'

For a time I just stare around in disbelief remembering how hard Mandy tried to make the flat homely with checked table-cloths, clean serviettes, and vases of flowers on the table. It seems kind of insulting to her to leave it in such a mess. So I find a big black dustbin bag and begin systematically to clear up. By the time my father comes back I have got rid of the rubbish, started the dishwasher, and made coffee in some reasonably clean mugs. There is no milk, but I have found some bread in the freezer and toasted it.

'Hey, that looks great!' He looks around the room in a bemused fashion as if I've done magic or something. 'How did you get to be so . . . ' He is lost for a word to describe my housekeeping skills.

'Intelligent people do everything intelligently,' I say with a frown. In fact, if I am honest, I have learnt a lot from watching Louie looking after the animals. When she is cleaning up after the puppies she always gets everything ready first: clean newspaper, an old feed sack for the pooey paper, a bowl of hot water, and an old rag. Then she moves the puppies out onto the grass and sets to work. It's no good talking to her when she's working, she won't look up or do more than grunt. It doesn't matter what she's doing, she really concentrates on it. I want to be like that and I'm pleased with the way I have tidied the kitchen.

'I'm going to go right through this flat and clean it up,' I say in a determined voice. 'Can't have Mandy coming home to a tip. I'll hoover and get some flowers and things and make it really nice for her.'

'Alex? I mean, that's very good of you, but . . . ' My father sips his coffee and frowns at me. 'I know you and Danny have always been close but . . . I mean I have wondered. What with you not having a girlfriend or anything.'

For a long moment I gaze at him, wondering whether to throw my coffee over him, then I decide it's not worth the trouble—I will only have to mop it up.

'It's just that if you *are*, that's fine by me . . . ' he starts again, giving me this really awful sly sideways look as if he thinks I might disintegrate at any moment.

'No wonder Mum divorced you,' I say slowly in a pained voice. 'You make assumptions about my sexuality *just* because I can clean up a load of filthy mess and do a bit of housework? For crying out loud I should think gorillas and chimps keep themselves cleaner than you do. What planet are you from? Have you turned being a slob into a full time career?'

'I'm sorry, Alex,' he says aggressively. He obviously isn't sorry. Just annoyed at being shown to be a pillock. 'But you must admit it is a bit odd. I mean seventeen and no girls and then going on like bloody Mary Poppins. "I'll get some flowers," ' he mimics nastily.

'Shut up and eat your toast,' I say wearily. 'I can't believe I come from the same gene pool as you.'

He doesn't eat the toast I have made, just drinks two cups of black coffee and then lights a cigarette. Then he scribbles something on a piece of paper from the telephone pad, the cig drooping from his mouth as he does so, his eyes squinting to avoid the smoke.

'This is the name and address of the hospital. Mandy is on Rutherford Ward. The service is planned for three o'clock. Mandy's parents are coming . . . I better get going. I've got to get into the office before the whole world falls apart.'

'Can I go to see Mandy this morning?' I ask.

He seems a bit surprised. 'Yes. I should think so. I suppose it would be all right. It's meant to be relations only—'

'Well, that counts me out, doesn't it,' I say rather bitterly.

'I should think they'll let you in. Don't go too early, will you?' he mumbles.

'No, I've got plenty to do here,' I say, sounding, even to my own ears, like some ghastly mother from a sit-com.

'Alex . . . ' My father's voice is weedling. 'If you could manage it, there *is* a bit of washing. Some stuff Mandy sent home from the hospital and my things. Could you put them in the washer?'

'Don't you know how to use the washing machine?'

'Yes, no. I mean it's so bloody complicated. I haven't

had much time . . . All this has been a hell of a strain on me too, you know.'

Looking hard into his face I don't think he looks worried, just fed up and a bit tense. 'Doesn't it get easier second time around?'

'No, it bloody well doesn't!' he snarls. Then he leaves, slamming the door. I sigh. That is definitely something I've inherited from him. I shall have to watch myself. I don't want to end up like my father.

The flat is so small it doesn't take me long to clean up. Everywhere is polluted with cig butts and empty beer cans. Everywhere, that is, except the tiny box room at the back, the room which Mandy had promised me when they moved to the flat.

When I first open the door I know I shouldn't go in, but I am unable to fight my curiosity. Everything in the room is new and freshly painted, as it should be for a firstborn child. There is a cot with lacy drapes and a diminutive chest of drawers. I shudder at the thought of what would have happened if I had accepted Mandy's offer and moved in here. It would have been like desecrating a shrine.

When I leave the flat I decide it's still too early to go to the hospital so I go to Mothercare and buy loads of stuff for the baby. I get completely carried away in there. First I get a frilly dress—all white lace and pink ribbons. It's the kind of thing I think Mandy will like. Then I choose a hanging mobile and an enormous teddy bear which is wearing wellingtons. It all comes to an absolute fortune and I spend just about every penny I've got on me. I have to count out my small change for my tube fare but I don't care.

It doesn't take me long to find Rutherford Ward. It is full of the sound of crying babies and I can't see Mandy anywhere. Eventually I ask this orderly who is mopping the floor. 'Last bay on the right, last bed,' she says, without looking up. As I walk down the long corridor I see that each bed has a clear plastic cot next to it. These cots are right next to the beds so the mothers can look at their babies all the time. Some of the cots are empty and the mothers are holding the babies, their nighties unfastened and the babies sucking at their breasts. I don't really know where to look, but no one takes any notice of me as I trudge along the corridor, the Mothercare bags banging against my legs.

Mandy has a bed next to the window. She is lying with her back to the corridor, facing the window, as if she's studying the sky and the clouds, but somehow I know she isn't. Her shoulders are humped with misery. There is no clear plastic cot next to her bed. The other three beds in this bay are empty. It is very quiet at this end of the ward, the crying babies disappear into the background of traffic noise and voices.

I tiptoe across the polished floor: 'Mand?' I say uncertainly.

She turns slowly. I've never believed those reports you read in *Reader's Digest* of people growing old overnight, but now I swallow hard and try to smile. Mandy looks like an old woman, her face is pale and creased, and her pretty, fluffy blonde hair is stuck to her forehead in lank strands. Her blue eyes looked bruised, full of some ancient hurt.

'Alex! I didn't know you were coming. I haven't washed my face or anything . . . I was just thinking about trying to get up.' She hauls herself up in the bed, like a beached whale searching for the ocean. I dump the bags on the floor and move forward to try to help her.

Sliding my hands under her arms I move her up in the bed and she winces. 'I've got awful stitches,' she says miserably.

'Stitches?' I echo stupidly. She smells of old perfume, and the warm scent of unwashed skin and milk. I sit on the edge of the bed. 'Where have you got stitches, Mand?' I ask concerned.

'Well, you know . . . down there,' she nods, a small

wan half-smile plays for a second over her mouth. 'I thought you learned all about it at school—babies and things.'

'Yeah . . . ' I say, thinking of the video we watched on childbirth. One of the girls fainted right away—but I thought it was all rather beautiful. The baby slid out like a lifeboat being launched, one good shout and whoosh . . . there it was, like some exotic flower fairy bursting from the swollen bud of a purple flower. There was never any mention of stitches.

'How many have you got?' I ask, puzzled.

'Oh, I don't know, hundreds I expect,' she says forlornly. 'Your dad will never fancy me again. He couldn't even stay in the delivery room. Was he there when you were born, Alex?'

'I don't know. I can't remember,' I say. But Mandy doesn't smile, she just looks sad. When her full mouth droops it looks just like a rose when the petals are about to fall. I want her to smile and suddenly I'm angry with my father.

'I shouldn't imagine for one moment that he was there when I was born,' I say forcefully. Thinking that a man who can't even use a washing machine would be pretty damn useless mopping up blood and afterbirth. 'And I'm sure the stitches won't make any difference.' Then, to take her mind off it all, I reach down and grab the carrier bags.

'Look what I got, for the baby.' I topple the bag and the dress and everything falls out onto the bed. 'And this,' I add, pulling out the teddy from another bag. I hold it out to her, I want her to take it, I want her to smile. But she just stares at all the stuff, then her hand comes out really uncertainly and touches the pink and white frilly dress.

'I bought it all in Mothercare. So if you don't like it, or it's the wrong size, I can take it back. I've got the receipt,' I say uncertainly.

'It's beautiful,' she whispers. And then she starts to cry. She starts really suddenly, like an engine which is switched on and immediately revved really high. She goes from nothing to great grieving sobs in about three seconds. I stand up, absolutely horrified, and stare at her. It's awful, her face is all screwed up and the sounds she's making are really deep and loud, like they've been torn out from right inside her.

I'm scared that someone will come and tell me off for upsetting her, because I suddenly realize that maybe buying all this stuff, dresses and teddies and things, is really, really tactless. If the baby dies then Mandy will have to take it all home and put it away in the tiny chest-of-drawers.

'Mandy! I'm sorry,' I say thickly, my throat aching with pain because I feel sorry for her, and sorry for myself because I've done such an awful thoughtless thing. 'Mand, please don't cry. I didn't mean to upset you. I shouldn't have done this. I should have thought. Please, Mand, forgive me.'

Kneeling at the side of the bed I take her in my arms. I hug her really close to me, stifling her sobs for a moment against the shoulder of my denim jacket. After a bit the crying lessens and I let go. She reaches for some tissues on the locker. I look away from her ravaged face and say again: 'I'm really sorry.'

'You haven't got anything to be sorry for,' she says, blowing her nose and mopping her face. 'It's not that . . . '

'I should have thought.'

'No!' she grabs hold of my arm. 'I'm glad you've bought her presents, though you must have spent an awful lot of your money. It's not that . . . It's just . . . ' Two more tears well and trickle down her cheeks, she rubs them away. 'It's just that it made me realize that you're the only person who has ever been pleased.'

She half turns away from me as she continues, her voice low and sorrowful.

'My mum and dad went mad when they found out I was pregnant. My mum said I was crazy to move in with your dad and have the baby. She kept on saying that I'd end up being a young widow.'

'Do mothers take special lessons on how to make tactless remarks to their offspring?' I ask wearily. Then I reach over and give Mandy another hug. 'You won't, though, Mand. You'll make a marvellous mum.'

'Do you really think so, Alex?' she asks beseechingly. 'You see, Steve wasn't really pleased either. He wasn't like my mum and dad, but I could tell. He's never been excited about the baby and my friends just thought I was stupid. But you . . . when you came to the flat, you were pleased. You were the only one that was. And I felt so awful about the room—your room.'

'Mand! It doesn't matter, honestly.'

'Would you like to go down to the special baby unit and see her?' Mandy whispers, her eyes large and luminous like giant forget-me-not flowers.

'Yeah. 'Course I would,' I say confidently. 'I've come to see both of you.' And I think this is what she wants to hear, because she gives this big sigh of happiness and rests her head on my shoulder.

'You know, I only started going out with Steve because of you,' she whispers. I stiffen, sensing danger. I don't know if I want to hear any more. Mandy is soft and warm in my arms and her voice is a sleepy drone. 'He used to tease me about you . . . saying you were sweet on me and that sort of thing. Then one evening he stopped at my desk and said: "You're too beautiful to be wasted on ignorant youths, come and have a drink with me this evening." And that was how it started.'

I don't know what to say: sorry seems inappropriate. Instead I just stroke her hair and keep my other arm tight around her. And she relaxes into my embrace, her body soft and pliant, her arms hanging on around my neck like she is a little kid who needs a hug. Anyone coming into the room would think we were lovers—but I don't care. I feel so darned sorry for her I could cry.

12

Going into the special care baby room is pretty exciting, because I have to get into a gown and mask and I reckon if I had a bleeper and stethoscope I could pass as a doctor. I begin to imagine a career in medicine, being part of a dynamic team like in *ER* or *Casualty*.

Mandy hobbles like an old lady, with one hand supporting her stomach and the other gripping on to my arm. Her tummy is still sticking out—it doesn't look as if she's had the baby—and I have to work hard at not staring because she looks so awful.

Really, I just want to close my eyes, and see her again as she was the first time Danny and I met her at my father's office; blonde hair all fluffed up and swung over to one side, wearing a short black skirt and a red blouse. Her lipstick matched the blouse and her velvet mouth was a scarlet streak against the pale cream of her skin. Danny and I had been utterly gobsmacked by how gorgeous she was.

'Gawd, your lucky pigging father,' Danny had said miserably when we got home. 'Fancy being in an office all day with that . . .'

'You'd go crazy, Danny boy! You'd never get any work done,' I'd joked.

'Too right, mate.'

'You'd end up looking like this . . . ' I'd crossed my eyes and let my tongue hang out, while doing a kind of idiot dance across the room.

'So would you, pillock-brain,' he'd said, and hit me on the shoulder. We'd ended up wrestling and cuffing each other all over the sitting-room floor. Now, when I look back, it was all a bit D. H. Lawrence, but it was our way of letting off steam.

It takes Mandy and me ages to shuffle along to the other ward. 'Are you all right, Mrs Harling?' the nurse in charge asks, concerned. 'You could have had a wheelchair.'

'Oh, no. I'm fine, really,' Mandy says, she seems a bit embarrassed about the Mrs Harling business.

'Let's find you both chairs to sit on,' the nurse says officiously. 'Then we'll get baby out for a change and a cuddle. Have you decided on a name yet?'

'I want you to choose the name,' Mandy says beseechingly to me. She looks like a frightened rabbit as she gazes at me, her eyes large and slightly vacant, as if she is overdosing on stress.

'Cool,' I say.

'Dads get all the good jobs, don't they?' the nurse says acidly.

'This is . . . this is my step-son,' Mandy stutters.

'Well, you can never be sure, these days,' the nurse says, her mouth puckering up as if she is sucking a slice of lemon. 'Strictly speaking only parents should be coming in here. I thought . . . '

'I wanted him to come,' Mandy says tearfully.

'My dad can't be here. He sent me instead.' I sit down quickly. Actually it is so hot and airless in the room that I feel a bit faint and wish I'd eaten more breakfast. Mandy sags down next to me.

The nurse says: 'Well, here she is and she's doing really well.' And she moves aside so we can see the incubator and the baby inside. There are only a few times in my life when I have been rendered utterly speechless and this is one of them.

Eventually, after a hideous pause, when the only sound is Mandy snivelling quietly beside me, I manage to say weakly: 'She's beautiful.'

This is so obviously a lie that the nurse manages a smile and says in an encouraging tone: 'Well done!'

'She's so small,' Mandy says miserably.

'Well, she'll get bigger,' I say reassuringly. I can't take my eyes from the baby—although I want to; she is small, red and wrinkly, her feet are too large for her matchstick legs and her head is oversized for her body. She is grotesquely dressed in a disposable nappy that is too big and a yellow knitted bonnet. Her chest has a tube attached to it by sticky tape in the shape of a cross—it brings a whole new meaning to cross your heart. The tube goes into her nose, maybe this is why her face is so screwed up and bad-tempered looking. No one would be happy with a tube shoved up their nose, would they?

'Are you going to hold her, this time?' the nurse asks Mandy.

'I . . . ' Mandy looks absolutely terrified. 'I feel so dizzy, say I drop her . . . ?'

'Come on now, Mrs Harling,' the nurse says crisply. 'Baby needs a cuddle.'

'I'll take her—I'm ace at cuddles,' I say firmly, and Mandy shoots me a grateful look.

'Maybe ''Mum'' will have more confidence if she sees you having a go,' the nurse says, frowning at Mandy.

Holding out my arms I remember saying to Louie how beautiful the puppies and kittens were and her replying: 'You should see 'em when they're born! All blind and hairless. Takes a mother to love them.'

As the nurse puts the scrap of humanity, which is Mandy's baby, into my arms, a moment of complete and absolute terror overtakes me. I have never been so frightened in all my life and I'm breathless with fear.

The nurse crouches next to me. 'All right?' she asks gently. Gradually air comes back into my lungs and my heart kick starts with a bound. I dare to breathe out. 'I'll stay here for a moment. Don't be scared to hold on to her.

She's not made of glass. Hold her close. It's good for her to hear your heart beating.'

'I'm OK,' I whisper. I want the nurse to move away and leave me alone. I look down at the tiny baby cradled in my arms, enthralled and repelled at the same time. She smells of antiseptic and stale milk, and some primitive animal instinct makes my nostrils twitch irritably. I know somehow that the other babies, the fat pink babies on the ward, do not smell like her, and this is the stench of the ill and sickly. I know now why Mandy didn't want to hold her. She is so fragile I find I'm watching her chest scared that each breath will be her last.

'You're the first one to cuddle her,' the nurse says encouragingly. And I am engulfed by a wave of sympathy and sadness for this scrap in my arms. It's as if no one wants her because she's so small and ugly, and it suddenly seems impossible that this little bag of bones could ever grow up to be a person. Mandy begins to cry quietly next to me, but I am lost to anything but the baby.

I'm getting used to her, growing comfortable with the size and weight of her in my arms, and I relax and gaze down with fascination at the nailless fingers and tiny hands. Her skin is so translucent I can make out the tracery of blue veins and the throb of her pulse fluttering in her wrist.

'Hey there, sweetheart . . . ' I murmur as if she is one of the kittens. 'What are we going to call you, eh, honeybunch?' I can't suggest we call her Faye. It would seem like a cruel joke to give that name to something so small and hideous. Also, I can just imagine my mother's incredulous smirk and Seth's clenched jaw when they were told.

'What would be a good name for you, little lady?' I ask the baby.

She doesn't have any eyelashes, her eyelids are just a pale purple line carved into the thin skin of her face. I am startled when the lids flicker and open a crack. I just snatch sight of her eyes; a glint of vivid blue, seen for a second like a kingfisher and then gone, leaving you with just a memory of colour.

'Hey, she opened her eyes!' I whisper to Mandy. 'She knows I'm talking to her. Say something to her, Mand.'

'I don't know what to say. I've never had anything to do with babies,' Mandy whispers miserably back to me.

My smile is sympathetic because I wouldn't have known what to say if I hadn't had the practice of talking to Louie's animals. Louie says that people who don't talk to animals are mad. I like that. I remember Louie pretending to be a mother cat and grooming the kittens with a toothbrush. 'They don't know they're alive if they don't have a bit of love,' she'd said.

Looking down again at the nameless baby I say a bit desperately: 'Hey, little sissy. In Yorkshire there is this great kid called Louie. How do you feel about sharing her name? We'll call you Louisa, shall we? What do you think of that, sweetheart?' Her eyes remain shut, but I'm sure she is listening, and so I murmur on for ages, just talking nonsense. Mandy stops listening and goes to sleep. The nurse moves off to check on the other babies and Louisa and I are left together.

'Time for her to go back in, we don't want her getting cold,' the nurse says.

'Goodbye,' I whisper. And, just for a second, as if she knows I'm leaving, one eye flickers open and she seems to wink at me. As the nurse takes her from my arms I feel a pain in my chest because I see again how frail she is, and I want so much for her to be pink and chubby, like the other babies.

'She will be all right? Won't she?' I ask the nurse.

'Yes, I'm sure she will. She's a real fighter,' the nurse says reassuringly. 'It's just a shame "Mum" has so little confidence.' She looks at Mandy, slumped and dozing in the chair, and her mouth folds into a disapproving line.

'She's just tired,' I say defensively, as I reach across to shake Mandy awake. 'She'll be fine in a little while.'

They put Louisa in a dress with a white knitted bonnet for the christening. I don't get a chance to hold her again and she doesn't open her eyes or anything, even when the vicar dribbles holy water on her head. She is so small and still it is hard to believe she really is alive. Mandy cries most of the time as does her mother. Her father and my father stand together, ill-at-ease in grey suits, both frowning. It's a miserable occasion by any standards.

As soon as we are out of the hospital building my father fishes his cigarettes from his jacket pocket and lights up. He sucks in the smoke like someone who has been drowning gulps down air.

'Why don't you give up?' I ask.

'Look, I'm meant to nag you, not the other way round,' he growls. 'Do you want a lift anywhere?'

'No. I'll get the tube. Could you lend me a fiver?'

He grunts and hands me a tenner. 'Will I see you this evening?'

'Maybe.'

'Could you get some beer and something to eat? I can't manage shopping . . . ' He hands me a couple of twenty pound notes.

'Remind me to tell you about supermarkets sometime. Everything you need for a civilized life is on a shelf. You choose what you want, pay for it and it's yours to keep. Quite simple.' I pocket the notes.

He walks off without replying which gives me some kind of satisfaction. I don't know why I feel so angry with him. I feel like tearing the cigarette from his mouth and stamping on it.

It takes me ages to get to Danny's house. I had forgotten how long it takes to get from one part of London to the other, all the hassle of going on the tube. I miss

Yorkshire suddenly, the cool air, the local bus, being able to walk down to Louie's.

As soon as I get to Danny's I realize I have arrived on the wrong day. They are going on holiday, the front hall is full of rucksacks and sleeping bags.

'Alex, old mate. It's great to see you. We're off to Sark first thing in the morning,' Danny says, punching my shoulder. 'Are you going to come with us?'

From behind him a girl appears: she is wearing a tie-dye dress, a droopy hand-knitted cardigan, and Doc Marten boots. She is too old to be a friend of Danny's sisters. I stare at her pale, nose-ringed face and long curtains of mousy hair. She stares back at me, there is some veiled hostility in her eyes which I don't understand. Silently she slips her hand into the crook of Danny's arm and tugs at him.

'This is Minny.' Danny's face is full of a mix of emotions: embarrassment and elation are in there and something else which I can't recognize. I hope it isn't pity. 'She's coming to Sark too. It'll be great if we're all there . . . won't it, Min?'

'Yeah . . . pleased to meet you,' she says slowly, holding out a limp hand to me.

'Bring Alex in for a cup of tea!' Danny's mum shouts. 'I've just taken some cakes out of the oven, come on in, Alex, and get indigestion.'

Danny's mum comes and gives me a hug and sits me down at the kitchen table. Danny and Minny sit opposite me and Minny keeps on touching Danny, as if to reinforce the statement: 'He's mine.' I can just imagine the fun we would all have camping together.

'Your mother phoned from Yorkshire and said you'd be staying with us in September. That's nice,' Danny's mum says, smiling at me. 'I've cleared the spare room out.'

'Thanks . . . ' I manage to say. But I'm so full of resentment towards my mother because she hasn't told me herself that I choke on my mouthful of rock cake and

Danny has to thump me on the back. Minny sits and stares at me like I've just arrived from outer space. After my choking the conversation turns to something else and I sit in silence, staring at my mug of tea, trying to work out why I feel so completely wretched. I have got what I wanted. I'm going to be staying with the Smiths in September. Every day I will go to school with Danny and come back here. Danny's mum will cook huge veggie stews and we will sit around the supper table like a proper old-fashioned family. But I know it won't feel right. It won't be the same as it used to be. You can't go backwards. And we have all changed during the few weeks I have been away. I don't know how I have changed—I just know I have. And Danny—well, Danny has Minny now.

To get away from them all I make excuses about shopping. The truth is I just want to get out, because the smell of curry and cats in Danny's house is driving me crazy. I marvel that I never noticed it before. I don't know how I am going to cope with living there, especially as September is the start of my A level year which means heavy-duty studying. As well as the smell the Smiths' home is so noisy: kids calling, the phone ringing, Mrs Smith shouting, the old man playing his old pop records in the sitting-room while he cleans motorbike engines. It's hell. My mother was right.

I stop off at the supermarket. More because I want to show my father up as an incompetent fool, than because I want to stock up the cupboards at the flat. Also it's something to do, something to take my mind off the complete loneliness of my life. I don't know what I am going to do with myself in September if Danny is still going out with Minny. I mean, we won't be doing all the things we used to do, will we? Snooker, swimming, and footie practice. It will all be out the window. Now it'll be going to see soppy films at the cinema and snogging. And I won't be able to go to my own home and get away from it. I won't be able to shut myself in my big spacious bedroom and turn my music up loud because I will be incarcerated in the Smiths' spare room. The prospect looms like a spell in solitary confinement.

Back at the flat I lie on the settee and watch TV until my father comes home.

'What do you want to eat?' he calls from the kitchen.

'Don't care.'

'We'll have a takeaway, shall we? Saves washing up.'

'No wonder your skin is turning yellow. It's too much nicotine and monosodium glutamate. And, as you don't wash up, that is a spurious argument,' I retort.

'Do you want Chinese or curry?' he asks.

'Don't care.'

He gets a curry. It's delicious but I can't eat it. The food seems to stick in my throat. Finally I put my fork down and look across at him. He's balancing his plate on his knee and frowning at the television screen, there is a trickle of red tandoori sauce running down his chin which he absentmindedly wipes away with the back of his hand.

'Mum's got in touch with the Smiths and said I can stay there in September. Did you know?'

'Yeah, thought you be pleased,' he says without looking at me.

'So she's definitely staying in Yorkshire, is she?'

'I don't know,' he says irritably. 'But the house is going to be sold.'

'Which house?' I echo stupidly.

'Which house do you think?' he replies waspishly.

'Our house?'

'Of course,' he says, with an exaggerated sigh.

'But I thought . . . Well, you said . . . When you left you said that Mum and I would stay there until I finished at school. I mean—that was the arrangement—wasn't it? A stable home environment for me, until I'd taken my exams.'

Just for a moment he turns and looks at me and there is scorn in his eyes. 'What is it with you kids today? I'd left home and was working by the time I was your age. I was living in horrible digs in Darlington and working every hour that God gave. Now you need your backsides wiping until you're eighteen.'

'I don't understand why the house has to be sold so soon,' I say mutinously.

'Because I can't afford two mortgages,' he says. 'I'm not King bloody Midas, and your mother spends all she earns on face cream and fancy clothes, hoping to hold back the tide of time.'

'Well, at least that's something you don't have to bother with,' I say, looking with distaste at the livid curry stains on his tie. 'You're an old wreck already.'

'Thanks, son,' he says, and belches softly.

'Anyway you don't have a mortgage on this place.'

'Mandy wants to move. She's been dragging herself all over Essex trying to find somewhere with four bedrooms which we can afford.' His voice rises with anger. 'Trailing around bloody estate agents when she should have been resting. All on account of you!'

'Why on account of me?' I snap, putting my plate down with a clatter.

'Oh, she thinks we need a room for you. I keep telling her you won't want to come within a hundred miles of us once you get away to university. You'll soon get yourself shacked up. But she won't listen.'

Closing my eyes to shut out his bad-tempered face, I imagine the scene. Mandy wanting everyone to be happy; wanting me to be included in a new house on one of the big housing estates so despised by my mother; searching for a box of a house with a narrow stairwell and three and a half bedrooms so that the smallest bedroom could be mine. I can even see the way Mandy would decorate it: a soft blue carpet, white walls, and lots of shelves. She might even buy a plaque for the door; one of those naff china ones from B&Q decorated with a football, a cricket bat, and my name.

'She probably wouldn't have started so early if she'd rested more. They warned her about her blood pressure,' he adds morosely, talking to the television screen and not to me.

'I don't know why everything is always my fault!' I say angrily.

'I didn't say that,' he says. 'Don't you go telling her I said that.'

'I'm going out. I'll see you later.'

'I'm going to the hospital. Have you got a key?'

'Yes.'

'Where are you going?' His voice is suddenly concerned.

'I'm going to see Danny and then on to the snooker club. Satisfied?'

He doesn't reply. I leave without saying goodbye.

But I don't do any of those things. Instead I walk the short distance to my old home. The FOR SALE board is leaning drunkenly in the front garden and I feel a kind of weakness steal up my body when I see it. I walk past the house, trying to look over the privet hedge without making it too obvious. All the curtains are drawn which is really weird. I walk along the street a couple of times and then I venture up the front path and look through the letter box. I know immediately that the house is empty because there is junk mail strewn along the hall carpet.

Inside my wallet I find my back door key. My mother told me to leave it for the tenants—I'm glad now I didn't. Opening the back door and walking in is really strange because it's our house, with our furniture, but it's full of other people's belongings. It's a bit like a nightmare walking around it, especially in my room because some American teenage girl is using it; the bed is draped with an enormous American quilt and there are pop posters and soft toys all over the place.

Out on the landing I investigate the door to the spare

room. It's locked with a padlock and all the stuff we didn't take to Yorkshire is in there. I find a big hammer in the garage and whack the padlock until it falls off onto the carpet with a soft plop.

When I open the spare room door and walk in I feel like Alice in Wonderland—suddenly I'm back in my world. There are piles of china and household stuff: duvets and cushions . . . all the things which I identify with home.

Working quickly and urgently I shift stuff until I have cleared the bed. It's the one I had as a child, a pine headboard, a narrow mattress, and the cover, yellow and black check, is the pattern I remember from when I was young. Sitting down I look at the muddle I have caused.

It's with a start that I realize I am looking down at a box which has my name on it. *Alexander*, written in felt tip in my mother's neat handwriting. I lean across and pull the flaps of the box open.

Inside is the story of my life; my birth certificate, immunization card, and passport are on the top, fastened with a metal paper clip and a piece of paper saying: Important Documents. Underneath are photo albums and piles of photos.

Tipping the whole lot out onto the rug I shuffle through. Right at the bottom of the box are a pair of blue satin baby shoes, and some nursery school paintings of abstract shapes in primary colours. Someone has written my name in neat letters and underneath these are my squiggles, pretend writing—so much for being a child genius.

Looking through the photographs I find that most are of my mother and me. A few are of my father and me, and only rarely, presumably when a stranger was coerced into taking a photo, are the three of us captured together.

In every photograph we look unhappy. I recognize it in the spaces between us, the odd gesture; my father's uneasy hand on my shoulder in one shot, the faraway look in my mother's eye in another. And in all the photographs of myself, including the school portraits, I sense a shifty restlessness. Were we a miserable family because of me? Was I the cause or the result? I really don't know, and wonder if they do.

I put my passport and birth certificate in my jacket pocket. That's all I need. Everything else I pile back into the box, throwing it in higgledy-piggledy, not nice and neat as it was before. Then I carry the box downstairs to where the Americans have built a barbecue at the bottom of the terrace.

After finding matches in the kitchen drawer I begin methodically to burn everything in the box. The photographs take really badly to begin with, but when I get a hot red glow going it eats everything up.

Finally, all that is left is black ash and charred remains, and glinting, like a white eye in the centre, is one of the pearly buttons from the baby shoe. I get hold of a stick and poke it out onto the flags of the patio. Then, when I'm sure it's cool, I pick it up and throw it as far as I can into the shrubbery part at the bottom of the garden, into a place where no one ever goes, not to weed or anything.

Although I'm tired out I don't feel like sitting down in the kitchen or sitting-room. Those rooms don't feel like my home any more and I feel like an interloper in them. So I go back to the spare room and make myself comfortable on the bed with a drink of water and the radio from the kitchen. The night is dark, it's really late, but I don't pull the curtains or try to sleep. Instead I lie down on the bed and look at the night sky through the window, thinking about Faye and wondering what she's doing. Then without knowing it, I fall fast asleep, the radio still playing.

13

In the morning I give up any idea of a career in medicine and decide that I'm destined to be a detective. The first thing I do is to check the diary next to the phone to see when the Americans are returning. The mother is as well organized as mine—there is a long arrow with HOLIDAY/EUROPE written in—which tells me they are due back in a week.

It's a weird and uncomfortable thought that this is the last time I will stay in this house. To take my mind off it, I lie on the bed and think about getting in touch with some of the kids from school and throwing a party. It would be fun to see them all again. I've been kind of lonely in Yorkshire. It's OK hanging out with Louie, but often I feel as if she's got other things on her mind. And as for Faye . . . a little worm of jealousy begins to uncurl inside me and turns my guts into a liquid fire. Now I'm out of the way there is nothing in the world to stop Faye getting it together with Leo Stanton. He obviously fancies her like crazy, who wouldn't?

And as for Faye, well, I just don't know. She is so even handed about people, always looking for their good side. It's one of the things I like about her. I hate girls who are always slagging people off. You know, even people they don't know like pop stars and people on TV . . . And the way some of them bitch about their friends! Honest—I'd hate to hear them talking about their enemies. And the things they say about boys! It's enough to make you celibate to hear the kind of intimate details they discuss.

My second-hand experience of schoolroom lust has

not been pleasant. When J-P, Danny, and I moved up into the sixth form, J-P fell in love with this dopey girl in our class called Petronella. She's really rough and has a hideous sidekick called Sofia. They are like a pair of clones: dyed black hair with purple streaks and nose studs like metal warts. Danny and I thought they were the ultimate pair of witches but poor old J-P got the hots for Petronella and eventually, after a load of ragging, she agreed to go out with him. It was, by all accounts, a disastrous evening, and afterwards, whenever J-P walked into the common room the two witches would start to waggle their tongues at each other and go off into fits of laughter. It was sick. J-P got really depressed and moved to a private college. I've hardly seen him since. Those two hell-hags are definitely not coming to my party and if they try to gatecrash I will turn them away.

Reaching into my rucksack for my Filofax I start to look up telephone numbers. Then I ring up a couple of people to ask what they are doing. There is a football special on tonight—I had forgotten that—and all the footie team are staying in. A couple of the guys ask me if I want to go around to their houses but I want to do something different. I want a party. But I start to feel desperate. J-P isn't answering his phone and Danny is away . . . I'm having a party and there is no one to invite. No wonder I've never bothered in the past. Apart from the football team I don't have any friends.

Searching the pages desperately I look for the phone numbers of girls. There aren't any. So I get out the phone book for our area. First of all I try the nicest girl in our class—Fiona Wright. She's Head Girl and one of those competent people who always knows what to do when someone faints or has a nose bleed. She'll probably offer to organize the whole party for me, right down to jellies and party bags. All I'll need to do is provide the space and a bit of booze. The phone rings for ages and no one picks it up and then finally a breathless voice says the number.

'Hi! Is that Fee?'

'Yes . . . ' She is panting and uncertain. 'Who is this, please?'

'It's Alex.'

'Alex?'

'Alex Harling . . . '

'Alex!' she says with relief. Obviously worried that she might have a crank caller or a heavy breather. 'How are you?'

'Fine! Look, I wondered, if you're not busy. I know it's short notice. But I wondered if you would like to come to a party at my place tonight? I'm back in London for a few days and I thought it would be great to have a get-together . . . you know, the old crowd . . . ' I'm talking too fast. There is a pause at the other end of the phone.

'I'd love to—but we're off on holiday. In fact we were just in the car when I heard the phone and rushed back in.'

'All right.' I am unrealistically disappointed.

'This isn't really a good time for a get-together,' she says kindly. 'Most people are away. Maybe the start of term would be a better time?'

'Yeah. I'll organize something later.' I get really depressed listening to her. She knows everyone's departure dates and what they are doing. I think of them all sitting in the sixth form common room talking about their holidays. Whereas I have nowhere to go and no one to see.

'Are you making a note of these dates, Alex?' Fiona asks rather sharply.

'Yes, I am,' I lie. In fact I'm doing a doodle on the telephone pad and thinking about how miserable I am.

'Now, Alex,' she says briskly, 'your best bet for a party would be the weekend before school starts. I'll ring and tell everyone, shall I? We can bring our photos.' She sounds really enthusiastic.

'Yeah, great . . . ' I say swallowing hard. I know I ought

to tell her that the house might be sold by then, but I can't be bothered.

'See you on the first of September,' she reiterates, as if I'm senile or something. When I put the phone down on her I feel a rush of annoyance flood over me. 'Stupid old bag,' I mutter as I make coffee. 'Who wants to have a party with Fiona Wright, anyway?'

Because I am so depressed I go to the shops on the High Road and spend all the money in my wallet on flowers and chocs for Mandy. It really makes me feel better. I can understand why people get addicted to shopping. Spending money stops you feeling lonely.

Mandy is really pleased to see me. 'How lovely of you to come to see me again!' she says, as she puts her arms around my neck and gives me a hug. 'It's so good of you to give up your holiday. You must have loads of other people you want to see. Are you going away somewhere with Danny?' she adds wistfully.

'Yes,' I say quietly. I haven't got the energy to explain about Danny and Minny. Or about how everything has changed and me not knowing where I belong any more. I don't want to spoil anything because Mandy is looking loads better. She has washed her hair and fluffed it up; and she is wearing pale gloss lipstick which makes her mouth look like a pink rosebud.

'Look, I got these for you!'

'They're lovely . . . And chocolates too!' I watch her blush. 'You're better than a husband, Alex,' she says shyly. 'Maybe I should have waited for you after all.'

I can't laugh, like I know I should. I feel too low. Everyone in the world seems to have someone apart from me. I start to wonder if Mandy would have *ever* gone out with me if I'd had the courage to ask her. But I know in my heart that this is lunatic talk. Even if she'd said 'yes' where could I have taken her? Out to McDonald's or for a walk in the park?

It's all right the old nurse thinking I'm her husband

now, when she's all worn out and drab, but what would people have thought if they'd seen us out together when she was a real looker? They'd have assumed she was my babysitter or my big sister.

'Shall we go and see Louisa?' I ask uncertainly. Part of me doesn't want to see her again. It's too painful to look at her skinny legs and the uneven rise and fall of her chest. But part of me craves another look at her.

'Oh yes! She's doing much better. I gave her a cuddle this morning. I kept on telling myself that if you could do it so could I. You put your dad to shame.'

'That's not difficult . . . ' I mutter.

Actually Louisa looks a whole lot better than she did yesterday. She has on a pink bonnet and looks more like a baby and less like an amoeba. 'Hello, sweetheart,' I say, as the nurse puts her into my arms. 'Pink is definitely your colour.'

There are two different nurses on duty today, no sign of old sour chops from yesterday. These two girls obviously think I'm an absolute scream. I put on quite an act: talking in funny voices to Louisa and telling Mandy jokes. I find myself basking in their laughter, their giggles make me feel unbelievably good.

'He's a real tonic. Isn't he, Mrs Harling?' one of them says. 'Is he going on the stage?'

The camaraderie of the hospital and Mandy's delight in my company lifts my mood until I get back to the house. I feel quite tired so I lie on the spare bed for the afternoon and read. By the evening I have finished Hardy's *Tess of the D'Urbervilles* and my mood has sunk into black depression. There's nothing like old Hardy for bringing on a fit of melancholia. I think about going back to the hospital to see Mandy, knowing that she will be pleased to see me, that she'll hug me with her plump white-skinned arms and tickle my face with her hair. But my father will be there. I don't want to have to share Mandy and Louisa with him.

It seems that everyone else in London, and the whole world for that matter, is having a great time—apart from me. I think of all the people in New York, Paris, and Rome who are going to parties or having intimate visits to the cinema with their partners. Danny and Minny will be together in their tent . . . whispering and kissing and having all kinds of fun which I don't even *know* about. Even Mandy will be having a cuddle with my father or Louisa.

In the end I feel kind of mad with rage, like you do when you lock yourself out of the house. It's so infuriating to be able to look through the windows and know you are only inches away from where you want to be. I feel like that about life. It's all happening and I can't get to it.

For a while I pace around the house. I really want to speak to Faye, but I'm scared. In the end I dial the number but there is no reply, the phone just rings and rings.

Checking my watch with the kitchen clock I see that it is still early and I wonder where Faye is and what she is doing. Thinking about her has made me feel sick and quite dizzy with longing. I want to speak to her so much I have a pain in my chest.

I start to feel quite poetic about how much this pain hurts when I realize that I haven't eaten much today. I can't remember if I had any breakfast, I certainly didn't have any lunch. My need for food has joined up with my need for Faye like the Space Shuttle linking up with Mir; and now they are both orbiting and crashing around in my solar system, causing havoc.

Just as I am about to return the phone to the wall I hear Faye's voice. I'm so overcome with delight that I slide down onto the floor and sit with my back to the kitchen cupboard, my legs straight out in front of me like a beggar. I say nothing. I just listen to her.

'Hi! Hi! Is that you Alexander? Alexander? Are you there?'

'Yes . . . How did you know it was me?' I whisper.

'I was thinking about you and wondering how you were doing. I was in the shower when I heard the phone. I know it sounds crazy but I just knew it was you. No one else would let the phone ring and ring like that.'

'Yes . . . You're right.' I'm knocked out by the sound of her voice. The room is spinning.

'How's the baby? How's she doing?' Faye asks.

'She's doing OK. Mandy asked me to choose her name.'

'Why, Alexander, that's swell. How lovely!' Faye sounds genuinely pleased. 'And what have you called her?'

'Louisa.'

'Oh . . . '

'After Louie. I thought it might help to give her the name of someone strong. Louie's such an original.' My voice trails off. The idea that some of Louie's courage might be magically transferred to poor ailing Louisa because they share a name doesn't sound so clever now. 'They've taken the tube out of her nose, she looks a lot better,' I add lamely.

'That's great news, I'm real pleased.' I sense a slight distance in Faye's voice. 'I'm sure Louie will be delighted when she finds out that you chose her name for the baby.' Faye sounds like a Sunday School teacher now.

Suddenly I blurt out, 'Faye, why don't you come down to London for a few days? We could have fun. I've got somewhere you could stay. Please come.'

Honest to God I had no idea I was going to say that. The words just appeared in my mouth because I want to see her so very much. I can't imagine not seeing her tonight, or tomorrow or the day after. I feel like someone who is drowning and grabbing at anything, even handfuls of water, in the hope of being saved. I don't know how I will carry on existing if I don't see her.

'Please, Faye, just for a few days . . . It would be fun . . .

Please come . . . ' I'm begging now. It's pathetic. I hate myself—but I can't stop.

'Alexander . . . ' Her voice is sorrowful. 'I'd love to. But I can't. I'm sorry.'

'It's that bastard Seth . . . '

'It isn't Pop, so please don't say that, Alexander. It's me. I promised Louie I would look after the animals for a few days. She's going away . . . '

'Louie, going away?' I know I sound incredulous. It's just I can't see Louie packing a suitcase and going away. Louie isn't a holiday kind of person—she wouldn't sit on the beach or ride on dodgem cars.

'She didn't tell me anything about it,' I say curtly. 'I can't believe she's going away. She's going to leave Fred . . . ?' I accuse and question at the same time.

'I'm sorry she didn't tell you about it, Alexander,' Faye says sadly. 'But she *is* going. And I said I would take care of everything for her. That's a big responsibility, Alexander, and it means I can't get away, not even for the day. I'm real sorry. I'd love to visit London with you. Maybe later in the holidays.' Faye sounds sorry, but she also sounds guarded.

'Where exactly is Louie going?' I ask, my voice steely. 'I can't believe she'd go without telling me.'

'I don't know precisely, Alexander.' Faye's voice is coolly grown-up. I'm obviously not going to be told anything else. I also know that if she's looking after the animals there's absolutely no chance of her coming to London. Disappointment makes my throat ache.

'What are you doing this evening?' I ask abruptly. I know that if I was really sensible I would not frame this question. I would just say goodbye and go back to the spare room and lie on the bed, licking my wounds like some injured creature who needs to be left alone. But I don't have a strong enough survival instinct to do that. I am like a lemming, rushing for the sea. And now I leap

161

over the cliff, rushing heedlessly to my destruction. 'Are you going out?'

'Yes, Alexander, I am.' Faye's voice is very gentle and calm. 'Pop and Diane are going to a party and I have been invited up to The Grange for supper. Octavia and Leo are having a few friends around. I thought it would be cool. It's kind of lonely here without you . . . '

I can't take any more. I stagger to my feet and replace the receiver cutting her off in mid sentence.

Suddenly I know I can't stay in this house any more. It seems like a jinx on me. What is the point of freeing myself from my past if I end up creeping back into my parents' house and living like a squatter? It's just too depressing.

There is no plan in my head as I pack up my rucksack and leave the house. I walk and let my feet take me. Eventually I find myself at the top of the High Road. In front of me is the Barley Mow. It is the trendy pub of the area, full of students and young people looking for a good time. All the outside tables are full and people are leaning in the doorway or sitting on windowsills. My pulse quickens, this is the nearest I'm going to get to a party.

As soon as I push my way into the pub and jostle my way to the bar I realize I have done the most stupid thing in the world. I have come into a pub with no money. I hunt through my pockets with mounting desperation, then I leaf through my wallet: there is my Livecash card, library ticket, various receipts, and rubbish—but no stray five pound note.

'Hell, hell, hell,' I mutter under my breath.

'Howay, lad, what's the matter? Forgotten your money?' A deep voice breathes in my ear. I shove all the stuff back in my wallet and crane my neck to look at the speaker. An enormous girl is standing behind me. She has a full moon face with small rat-like eyes. Although she's no beauty her smile is wide and friendly and I try not to make value judgements about her appearance although she does look seedy.

'You going to get a drink or what?' she asks pointedly. 'I'm parched, meself.'

'Yeah, you have my place. I've forgotten my money. I'll have to go to the cash point . . . ' I mutter, trying to squeeze around her. She doesn't move.

'Hang on there. I'll get you a half. Come and meet me mate.' Before I can reply she leans over my shoulder and waves a twenty pound note at the barman. She orders two halves of lager. 'What're you drinking?' she asks me with genuine concern. I am touched by this display of kindliness, so different to Londoners' lack of interest in strangers.

'That's very kind of you,' I say gratefully. 'I'll have a small lemonade shandy, please.'

'Well, you're cheap to keep and that's a fact!' she says genially, handing me a glass of icy beer and lemonade. 'Come on,' she adds, and I follow her through the crowd of people and out to one of the windowsills.

'Here's me mate,' the moon-faced girl says. I have to stop my mouth from dropping open because her friend is gorgeous. Small and dark haired, she has these amazing kohl-smeared emerald eyes surrounded by thick black lashes.

'I'm Jackie and this is our Jill . . . ' the big one says with a smirk. 'He's got no cash, poor lamb. Financially embarrassed until he goes to the bank! So I bought him a drink. Why, you could die of thirst before you get served in this place.'

'Hi, Jill,' I say.

'Well, hello,' Jill simpers.

'What are you two doing in London, then?' I ask, gulping my shandy. I'm hoping it will fill me up a bit. I feel ready to eat a beer mat I'm so hungry.

'We're going to go to the university . . . ' Jill says uncertainly, glancing quickly at Jackie, like a child looking for approval.

'Which one?' I ask. Jill looks flustered and doesn't answer.

'Why, London University, of course,' Jackie says, in a huffy voice.

'Right. And what are you studying?'

'History,' Jackie says firmly, as if this is the end of the conversation. 'And how about you? What are you doing with yourself?' she asks, and they both smile at me encouragingly.

'I'm taking A levels: English, History, Modern Languages, and Media Studies.'

'Eh! Quite a brain box!' Jackie jokes.

We are silent for a while, all sipping our drinks and looking at each other over the rims of the glasses. I wonder briefly why they are lying to me about being at university. Maybe they've come down here to work in tele-sales or something and want to make themselves sound more important. Thinking that, and knowing I owe them a drink, makes me feel really sad.

Now I have accepted the shandy I feel beholden to the girls. I hope I don't get lumbered with them. I begin to plan a getaway. But the thinking part of my brain keeps returning to Faye. I can't get her away from Leo Stanton by getting her to come down to London, so I shall have to go back to Yorkshire tonight or tomorrow. These thoughts preoccupy me to such an extent that for a time I even forget where I am or who I'm talking to.

The two girls ignore me but I'm aware of their chatter as they talk about pop stars. Eventually Jackie finishes her drink and goes back to the bar—it's time to make my escape. Smiling at Jill I put my glass down on the windowsill.

'Well, thanks very much. Nice to have met you . . . ' I say, sidling off. But Jackie taps my shoulder and as I turn around she thrusts another drink into my hand. This time it's a pint of beer.

'Come on, then, bonnie lad. Have a man's drink!' she says laughing.

'Actually, I haven't eaten today. I don't think I should
. . . ' I say hesitatingly, hoping she will offer to drink it
herself. The shandy has left a sour taste in my mouth. I
don't feel hungry any more, just ill.

'I must get going now . . . ' I say.

'Howay, lad,' Jackie says encouragingly. 'Just sup up
the beer I've got for you—'

The two girls stand next to me, watching me drink. I
feel like an animal in a zoo, or worse still a laboratory dog.
They watch as if it's part of a scientific experiment. When
I finish they both swig down their halves. We all stand
there with empty glasses. There is a silence which grows
ever longer and I realize that they have bought me two
drinks and I have no money and nothing to offer them in
return.

'Look, I'd love to buy you both a drink.'

They look across at me expectantly. Jill looks like a
little kid who has just been told Santa Claus is coming to
stay. 'Would you like a meal? There's a Chinese on the
Broadway, it's next to the bank. I'll get some money out.'
I realize that if I drink any more I'm likely to make a
complete idiot of myself. I'm desperate to get away from
the pub and have something to eat.

'That sounds lovely . . . ' Jill sighs blissfully.

'Come on then,' Jackie says. They walk one either side
of me, with Jill hanging on to my arm as if I might run
away or get lost. When we get to the NatWest Jackie
moves well away from me and starts looking in shop
windows, but Jill still swings on my arm like she's in love
with me or something.

'I've never had one of those card things, isn't it
grand . . . ' she murmurs, leaning over my shoulder and
breathing into the side of my face. I know I ought to push
her away and not let her see my PIN and everything but I
still feel dizzy and she is just *so* thick. I show her how to
ask the computer for your bank balance.

'Three hundred pounds, have you really got all that in

your account?' she says, coiling herself against me with the familiarity of a pet cat.

'Yes,' I say, as I turn away from her, reaching out to retrieve my card and money. But, just as my fingers fold around the crisp twenty pound notes, I feel this terrific bang on my back and I am knocked sideways and up. The force of the blow actually lifts my feet from the pavement. In a split second of terror I assume a car has left the road and wait for the sickening weight and the crunch of metal.

Then I am spread-eagled on the ground, with a terrible throb of agony pulsating from my jaw to the top of my head. It hurts like hell and my mouth is full of warm wetness. But the truth of my situation is more bitter than the salty blood in my mouth. I know that if I'm going to save my money I need to be up and running. But I can't move. I don't black out, but I come close to it. My ears are full of noise and rushing pain.

Slowly, very slowly, I roll over and sit up. Cars race along the Broadway and people are walking by, but no one takes any notice of me. An instinctive need to protect myself makes me stagger up onto my feet. I stumble over to my rucksack and fumble around, I need something to mop up the blood on my face. I wrap my dirty T-shirt around my head and find I still have one of the twenty pound notes, screwed up inside my fist. The other note, my phone, and my bank card have disappeared. I'm desperate to find a phone box and cancel the card, even though I know I won't be in time. There are loads of cash points nearby. Jack and Jill could have gone to Sainsburys or to the other end of the High Road. Jill knows my PIN and at this very moment they are probably in the process of drawing out my savings.

Through a fog of pain I remember that there are phone boxes at the tube station. Slowly, moving like a very old man, I hobble along to them. But my mouth is so sore, so full of blood, that the girl at the other end of the line can't make out what I am saying. Even though I know it's hopeless I repeat my details over and over again until she assumes I'm a hoax caller and hangs up on me.

Cursing aloud with frustration and pain, I replace the receiver. I can see my reflection in the mirror-like chrome on the front of the phone box. Even allowing for the distortion I look like the elephant man. I keep remembering that playground jibe: 'If you don't shut up I'll rearrange your features.'

With each second that passes my horror increases. I have lost my money . . . my face is a mess . . . But worst of all I know I can't go back to Yorkshire and face everyone. I am so ashamed of my stupidity I could scream and howl into the night. I begin to walk; movement is agony because it makes my face throb, but not moving is worse. When I stand still I have to think about what I have done.

Now I know I have lost I don't feel so angry with Jack and Jill. My rage is for myself. I have lived in London all my life. I know the rules like I know my own name. I have behaved like a complete fool. I walk on but I don't know where I am going—and I don't care very much.

14

My feet walk me to Jean-Paul's house, which is weird because I hadn't made a conscious decision to go there. Also, I don't normally walk when I visit him— I am surprised that I know the way without going on the tube. But somehow I manage it. I find I'm standing right outside his front gate, swallowing blood and breathing through my mouth because my nose is all blocked up.

J-P's house is very imposing and surrounded by a high wall with broken glass on the top. Set into the wall is a bell and an intercom—and just for a moment my courage fails me—because it seems impossible that a grubby, bloodstained youth with a rucksack could ever gain entry to such a place. Finally desperation takes over and I lean on the bell.

His mother answers. She has a beautiful voice, heavily accented like a French starlet: ' 'Ello, who is that please?'

'Aleth Arling. Jean-Paul's fwend.'

'Yes, just one moment. What did you say your name is, please?'

'Aleth . . . Aleth . . . ' I try again. What has happened to me that I can't get my name out?

Magically the gates part, and lights flash on, blinding me as I walk up the path to the open front door. From inside the house comes the sound of music and warm smells of garlic and hot food waft down the pathway to me. It is like a mirage because every step I take seems to carry me further away from it all. I can see J-P standing in the doorway but he seems to be growing smaller and smaller. When I am about halfway down the path he realizes something is wrong and comes rushing towards me.

'Alex! What ever is the matter? Mama!' he yells, his voice high and anxious. 'Fetch Papa! Quickly! Alex has had an accident.'

'Not an acthident. Jutht an abrupt meeting with a pavement . . . ' I slur out.

It's funny the things you can remember even though you are not aware of it. There I am, in old Jean-Paul's immaculate kitchen, bleeding like a stuck pig. And when his father comes hurrying in, carrying a black briefcase, I suddenly recall that he is a doctor. I have come to the right place.

For a while it's like *Casualty*. J-P's pa cleans me up and stitches my lip. He says that apart from bruising and a chipped tooth nothing else seems to be wrong. Wonderful man, he also gives me two enormous painkillers: 'Do I thwallow them?' I ask uncertainly.

'Take them with a glass of water, then tell us what happened.' Dr Arnold smiles.

'I'm thorry to dump on you like this . . . ' I mumble, gagging a bit as the tablets go down.

'You are lucky to catch us. We're off on holiday tomorrow,' he adds.

'Oh . . . ' Everyone is leaving London. Everyone else has somewhere to go—except me. I have no past—I burned it on the barbecue. And now I have no future. I can't confess to my parents, or worse still to Seth and Faye, what has happened to me. I feel strangely bereft knowing the Arnolds are going away. I've only just arrived. My life is like sinking sand at the moment, just when I think I might have a foothold it moves and disappears.

The Arnolds are very kind, they believe my story about having one too many in the pub and falling over the pavement. They also give me supper. Mrs Arnold has to put mine in the liquidizer because my mouth is so swollen. They don't expect me to talk or anything. I just sit, slopping food into my mouth, which isn't working too well because of the local anaesthetic, trying to get my head around what a complete prat I am. At the end of the meal it's really embarrassing because Dr Arnold suggests I phone my folks.

'I expect they'll be wondering where you are,' he says, nodding to the phone on the kitchen wall. They are eating their strawberries and cream, and Mrs Arnold is mashing mine with a fork.

First I ring my father, but of course he isn't there. Then I try Yorkshire. I know Faye won't be there—she is at the Stantons. And it is too early for Seth and my mother to be back if they are partying. But I try the number anyway and let it ring for ages. I wonder if Tiger can hear it and if he knows it's me. That thought, and if I am honest the thought of Leo Stanton breathing heavily over Faye, makes me really depressed and, to my everlasting shame, my eyes fill with tears. I suppose it's shock really from the accident. I brush them away hastily and wipe my nose on the piece of kitchen roll Mrs Arnold has kindly given me to wipe the dribbles of food from my chin.

'Nobody at home, Alex?' Mrs Arnold asks anxiously.

Shaking my head I explain: 'My dad's girlfriend's just had a baby, I expect he's at the hospital visiting her.' I see Dr Arnold's eyes stray to the clock on the wall. It's too late for hospital visiting. My father will be in the pub. 'He's probably gone out for a meal,' I add lamely.

'And your mama?' Mrs Arnold persists. 'Doesn't she have the answerphone, for the messages?'

'Not in Yorkshire. It's a rented place . . . she's staying with her boyfriend. They're out,' I say flatly, and I just catch a fleeting glance pass between Jean-Paul's parents.

'Maybe it's better for you to stay here with us for this evening . . . ' Mrs Arnold says comfortingly. 'The spare room is all ready. Those pills will make you very sleepy.'

She comes and sits next to me and puts the bowl of strawberries down in front of me, then she hands me the spoon like I am a toddler. 'Try to eat the fruit, Alex. I hope it won't sting your poor mouth.'

I would like to make some funny reply, they all seem so serious, but I can't think of anything. And after I finish the fruit mush my eyes start to close so J-P takes me upstairs to the guest room. I tug off my jeans and clamber into a gorgeous clean bed with heavy linen sheets. It seems an awful shame to get into such a lovely bed with smelly feet and a bloody T-shirt but I am too tired to shower.

My face hurts like hell in the morning and my mouth feels like it's stuck together with cotton wool. J-P brings me two more of the gigantic pills and a huge French bowl of fragrant coffee.

He stands at the end of the bed, looking at me a little uncertainly—my mouth is working better this morning but my hands are shaking like I'm a million years old.

'Alex, do you think it's possible you are having a nervous breakdown?' he asks quietly.

'No . . . ' I say. 'Why, do you think I am?'

'No . . . ' I wish he sounded more sure of himself. 'My parents have asked if you would like to come to France with us. They are going on to Italy, but I'm going to stay in France with my grandparents. I work on their farm—helping get the hay in and other jobs which are too heavy for them to manage. They are getting very old and it helps them to have an extra pair of hands for the summer. If you would like to come with me, you are very welcome. It's hard work—it might be good for you,' he adds.

'Well, you won't want me tagging along if you think I'm a nut case. Aren't you worried I will go off my rocker and murder you?' I retort sulkily. He's upset me suggesting I'm cracking up. I am entirely sane—just very much in love. I'd have thought J-P of all people would have understood that—but of course I haven't told him about Faye.

J-P smiles at me. 'I will enjoy your company, Alex. I'll go down and tell Mama you will come and she'll phone your father, if you like.'

I bet he doesn't mind having my company! I think bitterly, as I stand under the shower and wash my hair. 'What great practice for a would-be-shrink—his very own breakdown patient!'

For a couple of minutes I'm really angry and think about walking out of the house and disappearing. But then reality gets hold, because the options in my life are narrowing down. I have twenty pounds to last until September's allowance goes into the bank. I have nowhere to go and no one I want to see. I can't even go to see Mandy with my face like this. And the one place I really want to be, and the one person I want to be with, is out of bounds. Faye is locked, like a princess in a fairy tale, guarded by the twin ogres of Seth and Leo Stanton.

Suddenly I'm really fed up with life and with myself. I don't care where I go or what I do. And it is kind of J-P's parents to offer to take me to France. I decide to go with the flow, ride with the tide. I can pay back any money I borrow in September. After I have sponged the blood off my jeans and shaken the creases out of my T-shirt I go downstairs to face them.

J-P and me are like the guys in *Rain Man* during the ferry journey to France. I am the zombie and he looks after me. J-P's mum gives me mugs of coffee, sandwiches, and regular doses of painkillers and I shamble around next to J-P like Dr Frankenstein's monster. Most of the time we stay in our cabin, no point circulating and trying to pick up girls when you look like top-of-the-bill in the freak show.

'You don't have to hang around in here with me,' I tell

J-P miserably, worrying that even he might get fed up with being cloistered with an injured depressive all the time.

J-P goes off to the cinema. I could have joined him, because no one would see me in the dark, but instead I just lie on the bunk, cushioning my face and thinking about Faye.

'Would you like to borrow a pair of my jeans and a clean shirt?' J-P asks me when we dock in France. I suppose he's trying to tell me nicely that I smell. He's a couple of sizes bigger than me and his clothes hang off me.

J-P's mum smiles when she sees us disembarking. 'We will do a little shopping before we travel,' she says. We drive to a big hypermarket and she insists on buying me a pair of jeans, two T-shirts, and some arnica cream for my face. It all comes to an awful lot of francs but she just laughs when I worry about it. Her fussing makes me want to cry. It reminds me of Faye. I am glad my face throbs with pain all the time—it matches my rag-and-bone shop heart.

We drive south, and I awake in the back of the car to find that the light has changed. This part of France is soft, golden, and misty, and the air smells different, warm and spicy—as if the wind is coming from Africa. I go back to sleep, cocooned in a whiteout of pills, my head on J-P's shoulder and a tartan travel rug over my knees, as if I am an elderly invalid being taken someplace to die.

J-P shakes me awake. 'We have arrived, Alex.'

I step from the car. There is an old stone house surrounded by a garden full of sunflowers and two barns with ancient bowed roofs. I blink as the colours hit me: the soft green of the grass, the gaudy yellow flowers, the vivid blue of the sky and a wonderful patchwork of orange lichen on the amber roof tiles.

The grandparents come rushing out to greet us and there's lots of shouting and kissing—real high octane excitement. J-P is patted and hugged like he's a young god just stepped down from Olympus, and his *grandmère* insists I stoop down so she can kiss me too. She talks so quickly, and has such a strong accent, I can hardly make out what she is saying, but she flutters around me like a little welcoming bird.

'Come and have some breakfast . . . ' J-P says, as we share a smile.

Downstairs there is a big living-room with an old fashioned cooker and a scrubbed table. We all sit there dunking rolls into bowls of coffee while I respond to their questions with my stilted schoolroom phrases.

'*Grandmère* will look after you and find you something useful to do,' J-P says when the car has been unpacked. 'Everyone is busy here.' It's not a complaint or anything. It's a statement and makes me feel like I'm wanted.

Grandmère gives me lots of jobs: I pick peas from the garden and sit in the sunshine by the back door shelling them, then I peel and cut up vegetables and turn the handle of the butter churn. It is very soothing and restful. The old lady supplements all her instructions with elaborate mimes and lots of encouragement, obviously assuming that because my French is so bad and I look so weird I must be half-witted.

The following day I graduate to weeding the garden. *Grandmère* gives me a little fork which I use to lever away the baby dandelions and other weeds which are smothering the onions. Surprisingly I find that I enjoy clearing the ground, leaving the onions standing tall and proud in a sea of dark rich soil. I break up the fertile French loam with my fingers, playing with it like a kid at the seaside.

The day after that I am considered rested enough to go out with J-P and his grandfather to do men's work. J-P's *grandpère* is very old, with a face as brown and wrinkled as a walnut and dark, sad eyes like a basset-hound. He doesn't speak much to me, and sometimes I sense his gaze on me, puzzled and somehow dismissive. It makes me determined to work hard and show him I am not a shirker.

J-P is very different to how he is in England: he doesn't talk much and seems preoccupied. After our first morning of work I know why. He hasn't the energy to be convivial—we need all our strength for the work. J-P's *grandpère* may be as old as the hills, with a bent-over back and arms as thin and sinewy as rigging ropes, but boy, can he work!

At lunch time *Grandmère* looks at me anxiously and chatters away.

'*Grandmère* says you should have the afternoon off and she will find you something a bit easier to do,' J-P explains with a wry smile. 'She's worried we've worn you out.'

'I'm OK,' I protest. I am loath to admit I can't keep up with him and the old man. I keep telling myself that hard work never killed anyone, but by the end of the day I'm not so sure about it. My shoulders are stiff and aching and my eyes feel as if they might pop from their sockets from all the lifting and carrying.

'We will be haymaking for the next week while the weather holds. Then there are the early apples to pick,' J-P says, watching my face for any signs of imminent breakdown. I manage a smile.

'Great!'

'It's funny. I never thought of you as the outdoor type,' J-P says. I am too tired to argue. It wouldn't be so bad if there was a proper bathroom and I could have a long hot soak and unknot my muscles. But all the grandparents have is a funny old hip bath thing and a shower. I think they are quite poor. There aren't any carpets in the house, only rugs, and the food they eat is very simple: fish and soup and bread . . . And the beds make the cottage in Yorkshire seem luxurious. I like it though, it fits in with my mood that I shouldn't really be enjoying life.

That evening I call my mother. When the phone starts to ring I pray that Faye will answer. I just want so much to hear her voice—even though I don't know what I would say to her. But it is Seth who drawls out the number.

'Can I speak to my mother, please?' I say formally.

'Hi there, Alex! How are you doing?' he booms at me.

'Very well, thank you . . . ' I say, scowling.

'Alex! Are you having a good time?' my mother asks. 'It was such a surprise to hear you were off to France. But Jean-Paul's mother is simply charming, isn't she? And she said it was no trouble and you would be company for Jean-Paul. It's nice, isn't it, that you've kept in contact with him and are such good friends.'

She makes it sound as if I am some social misfit who never bonded with anyone. I suppose what she really means is that J-P comes from the right kind of social class, whereas Danny never counted as a friend because he lives in a council house.

'Is Faye there?' I ask sulkily.

'Oh no! We never see her these days, she's always out . . . ' My mother's laughter tinkles, false and cruel, down the phone line.

'I've got to go,' I say miserably.

'Oh, darling! Tell me about the place where you are staying. Is it lovely? Mrs Arnold said it's a farm.'

'Yeah, we're right out in the country—lots of animals and rats as big as cats in the yard. But it's all right because they're superior aristocratic rats.'

'Alex!'

'I'll phone next week,' I say, and hang up. Faye is always busy, always out. I am so pleased I'm not there, even though I miss her. I have a sudden vision of myself waiting alone in the Yorkshire cottage, listening for the sound of Leo Stanton's roaring MG to pull up outside. Thinking about this image makes me really hysterical. I insist that J-P and I walk to the nearest village even though it's miles and my legs are weak from raking hay.

We sit outside a café drinking ice cold beer and watching a group of old men playing boules in the square.

We are too tired to talk and after two drinks we walk home. I only just make it—my legs feel like overcooked spaghetti.

'I thought France was meant to be full of beautiful girls. We haven't seen a single one,' I grumble to J-P, as we arrive back at the dark and silent farmhouse. I want to snog a French girl, even an ugly one that reeks of garlic would do. I want something to drive the thoughts of Faye and Leo Stanton out of my mind.

'Oh, shut up, Alex. We'd be too tired to do anything with beautiful girls, even if we could find them,' he says with a grim smile. And then he adds with a little laugh: 'I told you coming here would do you good.'

The work continues and the days merge into each other in long sunlit hours of grafting and sweat. Only Sunday is different because the grandparents get dressed up and go off to Mass in the morning and we do only essential jobs in the afternoon.

The rest of the time it's one long endless round. Among other things I learn how to cut, rake, and rick hay, to pick apples and make cider, to creosote fences and milk cows. I sometimes wish, when I have time, which isn't often, that Louie could see me because I have become a pro. If I was dumped in the Western Desert, or the Canadian Rockies, I bet I could build a cabin, chop wood, shoot a moose, and survive. I'd really like to send Louie a postcard and tell her what I am doing, because I know she'd be impressed, but I realize I don't know her surname or address.

The one great advantage of hard work—physical work—not book reading and chattering about things—is that it dumbs your mind. All you think about is your next meal or how splendid a bowl of coffee and a hot bread roll will taste. You forget about everything else.

Hard work changes something else too—*Grandpère*'s expression is different when he looks at me. Sometimes when we are working he starts the job and then hands me the axe or the paintbrush with a little shrug and a smile.

'He doesn't want to admit it but it's getting too much for him,' J-P tells me. 'It's been good to have you here, Alex,' he adds. I like that. It makes us seem like comrades. And I realize that even without many words being spoken J-P and I are closer than we have ever been.

15

The next Sunday evening, after the grandparents have gone to bed, J-P and I sit in the cool of the garden and drink a bottle of wine. 'Are there any classy girls at your new college?' I ask.

J-P shrugs. 'Some of them are OK, but there's no one I feel that vital spark for, like I did for Petronella. Was there someone special in Yorkshire?' he asks.

I am silent for a moment. What can I tell him about Faye? Not so much a vital spark, more a raging forest fire. And what did I do about it? I blew it. I got jealous and acted like a kid. The worst thing is I never even got around to kissing her or showing her how I felt. It is a story of ultimate failure and humiliation.

Words fail me. Instead I tell him all about Louie and the great times we had together. I just mention Faye in passing. Not that you can pull the wool over J-P's eyes—reading all that Freud and Jung has really given him an edge.

'So, Alex, Louie is a great mate—but what about the other girl—Faye?'

'Well, she's American . . . ' I say a bit lamely.

'Yes, you've already told me that,' J-P says, laughing.

I throw the cork from the wine bottle at him. 'She's bloody lovely . . . ' I mutter thickly. 'But if she goes back to America I'll probably never see her again.'

'Well, do something about it then, Alex. If she's that special don't just let it go,' he advises. 'Why don't you write to her?'

But what do I write? Me—who has always been so

good with words—spends hours looking at a blank page and then can only write in block capitals like an illiterate. I LOVE YOU FAYE. Crazy man!

The next day there is a letter for me. I don't recognize the writing. It's in a pink Forever Friends envelope and my hands shake a bit as I open it. J-P deliberately looks away and doesn't josh me.

It's from Mandy. A newsy letter full of how much Louisa weighs and how many times a day she is feeding. Also my father has learned how to change a nappy. What a pigging miracle! Tucked inside the notepaper are two photos of Louisa. She looks like the skinned rabbit *Grandmère* prepared yesterday for Sunday lunch. This likeness doesn't escape *Grandmère*, when she sees the photos she wails a bit and dabs her eyes. Then she takes the pictures and reverently places them around the statue of the Virgin Mary, which is kept on a half-shelf in the living room.

'*Grandmère* says she will say special prayers for the poor little baby,' J-P tells me.

The next day I feel a bit uncomfortable when I notice that this impromptu shrine is hung with rows of glistening rosary beads, a small pink candle, and a posy of fresh flowers in a tiny glass of water. It seems like black magic. But this invocation seems to work. When the next letter and photos arrive Louisa has improved no end. She actually looks like a tiny golden-haired doll.

Grandmère is very excited by this improvement and there is much kissing and hugging of me and J-P, and an extra special display of scented flowers to carpet the Virgin's feet. I am tempted to ask whether *Grandmère* could put a love spell on me and Faye, and turn Leo Stanton into a stag beetle for a while, but my French isn't up to it. Anyway she might be offended.

Instead I walk to the post office and send a huge postcard addressed to 'Mand and little-sissy-Lou-Lou' because I know it will drive my father bonkers.

No one else writes to me. So my only other pleasures are waking in the morning and hearing the larks sing, or sitting in the cool of the evening and drinking the raw vinegary wine the grandparents have with supper. These pleasures are transient and do not trouble my mind. I don't want to write poems about them. I just want to enjoy them. And most of all I want to rest.

I remember a kid from junior school days. His name was Benjamin and no one ever shortened it. One day we had to write a prayer and read it out to the class. Benjamin was the last to read, probably because all he had written was: 'God Bless My Bed.' The whole class cracked up and our teacher got really annoyed and told us God was just as interested in short prayers. Anyway . . . good old Benjamin. I wonder what he's doing now. I think about that prayer at night as I punch my square pillow into shape and zonk out. I sleep so deeply here I don't even dream.

Sometimes I think about not going back to England, of staying here, because I feel peaceful in a way I've never done before . . . but in the back of my mind, dampened down by hard work, but not extinguished, is my need to see Faye. I've got to see her—even if it hurts like hell. If it wasn't for her I wouldn't go back.

Anyway, J-P's parents arrive for us, and it would look pretty silly refusing to leave. I mean, the grandparents and I are great friends—they even make me promise to come back with J-P next year—but they haven't offered to adopt me or anything. So I get together the bits of clothes which are all I've got with me and we start the journey home.

By the time we reach the grey blur of London I am so desperate to see Faye I refuse the offer of a night at J-P's. Instead I borrow the fare and catch a fast train to Yorkshire. As the train pulls out of King's Cross I feel quite giddy with relief. London is full of obligations: school, Danny, my father. But doesn't feel like my home any more. I know I will have to pick up the threads of my life soon enough—school term begins in a week and I have to take my A levels—but for today I can escape.

No one sits next to me on the train probably because I look so scruffy. My hair is too long and I'm wearing the clothes I left Yorkshire in all those weeks before. My jeans are nearly white from frequent washing and drying in the hot French sun.

The fast train takes me only as far as York and it takes ages to get from there to Yarham and even longer to get out to Gouthgill. It is late afternoon by the time I arrive. I realize I will have to stay the night and wonder what kind of welcome I will receive.

It is strange to be back in Yorkshire. It seems very green and clean and cool. I miss the warmth of France and the long hours of sunshine. Shivering, I get my thick shirt out of my rucksack and put it on. Then I walk quickly down through the avenue of trees past the long sheet of blackish water.

The weeks I have been away seem to vanish with each step I take. Everything here looks familiar and well-loved, much more so than London did. Yet I lived in London for years and years and was only here for a few weeks. I suppose I was happy when I was here—and that is why it is all imprinted so favourably on my mind.

But even though it's great to be back and see it all again, I realize that this isn't my home any more than London. If I am happy to be back it's because Faye is here, just as I would treasure anything which was connected with her.

The truth is I don't feel I belong anywhere—except where she is. It's a bit of a scary thought that home isn't a physical place—but is where your heart is.

When I can see the cottage I have this insane desire to yell Faye's name at the top of my voice and do a bit of a Heathcliff. Poor old Heathcliff—everyone thinks he was such a bastard, but he didn't have a proper family or a home either. No wonder he couldn't forget Cathy and kept on going back to her like a homing pigeon.

I know how he felt. I want to see Faye so much I feel delirious. All these weeks of keeping thoughts of her at bay have left me with a backlog of emotion, so I'm suddenly crazy with longing. I don't care what she has been doing. I don't give a stuff about Leo Stanton. I just want to look at her again, hear her voice, and be in the same room as her for a little while.

The cottage is empty . . . There is cat food in the kitchen but no sign of Tiger. No one to welcome me. I feel quite choked with disappointment as I look in all the rooms, searching for any signs of Faye. There's precious little to find. I get the feeling she hasn't been here for ages.

Leaving my rucksack in the kitchen I go down the lane to Louie's. At the gate Fred welcomes me and nuzzles my pockets.

'I'm sorry, old mate. I haven't got anything for you,' I explain. He doesn't seem to mind, he just seems pleased to see me and he follows me slowly up the hillside. I shorten my pace so he can keep up. He is slower now and more lame, but he seems very alert and nudges me in the back like he used to do. 'Well, at least you're pleased to see me, Fred, old man.'

The sheds are as neat and clean as ever. There are no puppies or kittens, just the old man pheasant and a brown hen with some chicks. There's no sign of Louie. The chimney of the cottage has a plume of woodsmoke trailing into the sky and I can hear the sound of children's voices, but I don't like to go up there. So I sit down on a wooden box and wait.

Evening falls. There is a feel of autumn in the air and soft curling fingers of mist begin to rise from the lake. Desolation fills me. Maybe I won't get to see anyone, not even Louie. I'll just collect my books and go back to London with an empty heart.

As I move to the doorway I hear a bark, it isn't

Blue's bark, it's the high pitched yap of a puppy pretending to be a guard dog. A small black and white mongrel of dubious ancestry, but with a lot of sheepdog in it, rushes up and starts jumping up at me, barking in a frenzy. I manage a smile because I'm sure it's my puppy, my favourite who I used to cuddle. I'm pleased Louie has kept him.

I hear a voice call: 'Wolf! Wolf, come here, good dog . . . ' And I start to laugh as a small figure appears and runs down through the trees. It's a girl wearing grubby jeans and a man's shirt but it isn't Louie—it's Faye. I hold out my arms and she rushes into them.

'I don't know why I'm hugging you, Alexander Harling! You bad boy!' she says, pulling back from me and surveying me with a mock frown. 'All these weeks and not even a postcard! For someone who is going to be a writer that is pretty darned poor!'

'How do you know I want to be a writer?' I ask, desperately trying to hide my pleasure at the sight of her.

'Your mom is forever boasting about you, and showing us all the stories and poems you've had published in the school magazine. She said you were going to try for journalist school. I sure hope you don't need to write letters home as part of the course!'

'I'm sorry. There was nothing really to write about . . . ' I can't stop looking at her; her hair is tucked behind her ears, her face is covered in freckles and there's no sign of earrings or nail polish. In fact her hands that are now holding mine are as brown and rough as a boy scout's after a fortnight at camp. She looks like a scruffy kid in her torn jeans and oversized shirt.

'Where's Louie?' I ask. Her face changes, she pulls her hands away from mine nervously and reaches down to pat the puppy. 'Fred's looking good,' I add. 'I'm surprised he's still with us.'

'Yes, he's doing fine . . . And there is a new baby kid. It's so cute! I've just milked the goats and taken them up to a pasture at the top of the lane. They've eaten every blade of grass in the churchyard. I'm walking miles to find them something to eat.'

'Why are you still looking after them? Where's Louie? Is everything all right?' I look down at her tanned face and broken nails with puzzlement. 'You look as if you've been working hard all summer.'

I see Faye steel herself and then she says quietly: 'Louie's been away all summer. She joined a demo. They're fighting to stop a new road being built through a wood. There's a gang of them living there in a camp to stop the bulldozers moving in. They've been on the TV News and everything.'

'Great! Sounds just Louie's sort of thing,' I say with a grin. 'It's good of you to look after the animals for her. And you kept this little 'un. He was always my favourite.' I bend down to pat the puppy because I am trying, without making it too obvious, to look into her eyes. I don't understand why she's so upset.

'Is everything all right with Louie?' I question.

'Yes, she's fine.'

'And Blue?'

'Yes, he's fine.' Faye looks away into the distance, as if the valley is suddenly very interesting. 'Louie is living in a tree house.'

'Brilliant.'

'Yes, she's sharing with a friend . . . '

'Yeah, well, it must get a bit lonely, mustn't it? Being up a tree on your own.' I laugh but Faye doesn't join in.

'She's sharing with a boy, he's called Ace.'

'Freaky! But that's not much of a name for an eco warrior, is it?' I say in mock horror. 'Ace! Makes him sound like a professional gambler. I thought they were all meant to be called Marsh or Fen or Hawk, something suitable to their lifestyle. I suppose Louie's just thankful he's not called Great Tit or Corn Crake.' I'm desperate to make Faye laugh, but she won't even smile at me.

'I'm sorry, Alexander,' she says glumly.

'Why are you sorry?' Slowly it dawns on me. 'You don't think, you didn't think . . . well, I mean, that Louie and I were . . . you know?'

'Of course!' Faye's eyebrows lift. She almost looks grown-up again. 'You were so annoyed when she went away without telling you. And you named Mandy's baby after her.' She looks upset, her eyes fill. 'I thought it was such a lovely gesture. I thought she'd be so thrilled. I know I would have been.'

'Knowing Louie she probably went "Humph",' I say miserably.

'Yes—she did. And the day after you left she turned up with this boy. He's very strange . . . he dresses in black leather and bondage chains. I was really upset for you when they went off together.'

'Really, there was no need,' I say abruptly. 'There was never anything like that between Louie and me. We were just good friends.'

At last she smiles at me with relief. 'Oh well, that's one problem out of the way.'

I get this terrible premonition that she has something else to tell me that I'm not going to like. I swallow hard and ask: 'And how are the Stantons?' I am concentrating on stroking the puppy's ears. He is ecstatic with all the fuss and rolls over on his back.

'They're having a great time in Florida.'

'FLORIDA!'

'Yeah, people do go there on holiday, you know.' Faye looks at me with a puzzled frown. 'They take a house on Marco Island during August. Mrs Stanton has relatives in the States and they all meet up there. It sounds great. It must be marvellous to have a huge family gathering like that.' She gives me a meaningful look and adds, 'I've had two letters from Octavia and three postcards from Leo while they've been away.'

'He obviously thinks you need reminding of what

Florida looks like. Have you sent him a postcard of Yorkshire? He might forget where he lives.'

Faye gives me a stern look: 'I don't know why you've always had a down on Leo. He really is a charming boy.'

'Especially when he's on the other side of the Atlantic,' I mutter. Actually I'm furious with myself because I could have spent a whole precious summer here with Faye. Instead I've hidden myself away in France just because I was too uptight and stupid to find out the facts. Old Thomas Hardy could have written a great book about me . . . He would have called it *The Fool of Gouthgill* or something like that.

'Alexander! I'm just so pleased to see you,' she says in a rush. 'There is something else. I suppose I'd better tell you.'

'Come on then, spit it out,' I say uneasily. Her anxious mood is infecting me. I feel really edgy and nervous.

Faye takes a deep breath. 'Seth and your mom are going to get married.'

'It was nice of them to let me know!' I say moodily, turning away from her. Despair fills me. I'm going to be lumbered with Seth—but what's going to happen to her? I am scared she will tell me she is going back to the States and my world will end completely.

'Oh dear! I was worried you wouldn't be pleased when you heard,' she cries mournfully. 'They only decided like days ago. No one knows but me. I think they wanted to tell you face to face and not over the phone. Please, Alexander, don't be angry.'

'I'm not angry. I don't really care very much what they do. It won't make any difference to me,' I say miserably.

Faye gets hold of my arm and pulls me around: 'I really hoped you might be pleased for us,' she says tearfully. 'I thought . . .'

It really hurts me to see her upset. I reach across to her and pull her towards me. Then I wrap my arms around her as tight as I can, like she's a teddy bear and I'm a little child. I had no idea it would be this easy to get close to her. It's as if we have always hugged like this. As she nestles into my chest, I ask quietly: 'What did you think? Come on, tell me.'

'I thought it would be so wonderful for us,' she whispers. 'You see, my parents have agreed I can stay in England. And that means you and me can be together whenever we want. No more being *einzelkinds*. No more Christmas and summer holidays alone. We're kind of special when we're together, aren't we, Alexander?'

My breath comes out in a sigh as her arms slip around my waist. She hugs me with unexpected strength.

'Yes,' I say quietly. 'And just for you I will try to forget I hate Seth's guts. I'll be the perfect member of the perfect family. I won't do it for anyone else.' And I think she knows what a big deal this is for me, because she gives this little cry of joy.

'Oh, Alexander, it makes me so very happy to hear you say that.'

'Yeah,' I whisper. 'I think I'm happy too . . . ' And I am! It's such a strange feeling that I wonder if I have ever been really happy before. I feel like I've just been born again. Suddenly everything is different. I am here—but not alone. I have Faye next to me. And I really don't care what the future holds, as long as I am able to share some corner of her life. Happiness makes me feel expansive and strong. I begin to make promises to myself—how I will always look after her and be around if she needs me. And how, one day, I will write down just how wonderful it is to have found her and make it into a book.

Bending my head I snuffle in her hair, breathing in the warm scent of her, deliberately holding back, savouring the long moment before I kiss her for the first time. Then I spoil it all by laughing.

'What's so funny, Alexander?' she asks, as she presses her face against mine.

'Nothing, I'm just happy,' I whisper. I wouldn't dream of telling her that she smells of goat.